THE

Blasted

TOWER

◆ FriesenPress

Suite 300 - 990 Fort St
Victoria, BC, V8V 3K2
Canada

www.friesenpress.com

ISBN
978-1-5255-4321-0 (Hardcover)
978-1-5255-4322-7 (Paperback)
978-1-5255-4323-4 (eBook)

1. FICTION, ROMANCE

Distributed to the trade by The Ingram Book Company

THE
Blasted
TOWER

Coming into Wisdom

CATTI-ANN BELLE

PART I

The Winds of Change roll upon us
With gentle hands or brutal force
They always leave their mark
Go forward from there, the Angel sings
Embrace in your heart this brand-new start
And feel the love that it brings

The Winds of Change

CHAPTER
I

Andee could feel the new days' warmth beginning to emerge as she ran along her tiny part of the expansive California coast. The heat of the day was just beginning as the sun perched on the horizon with the dawn.

She could feel the breeze cooling her heated flesh. Her heart raced from the exertion while her feet pounded the sandy beach. She steadily jogged back toward her private oasis nestled in amongst the rocks along the beachfront.

Her spot contained a simple, solitary bench within a temple of rock located in front of her beachside home. This was her favourite place to sit and ponder. Her home proudly protruded high above her oasis.

Today she was again imagining the breeze as a sheer, silky robe that caressed her arms and legs in a beautiful white splendour that only an angel could provide. This robe would become her wings that allowed her to float ever upward as she moved along. She didn't feel like she was running—she was flying along, her feet never touching the sand.

Moving higher and higher, she could feel the robe stretch beyond her as it carried her to the sun. It was moments like this she felt the most peaceful, within the quiet of her imagination before the reality of her day took hold.

She felt her body move fluidly, the grace and precision as one foot landed and the other took flight, propelling her ever forward. Her arms worked as they always did, back and forth in perfect rhythm with her legs, every muscle of every limb automatically doing what it did best. She was moving in flawless harmony while her thoughts floated away.

She didn't run to stay in shape. Her motive for running every day was the escape and the fact that she could still run. Also, she loved the freedom that came with it.

She ran every morning until she reached the point where the sandy beach ended before turning around to head back to the beach in front of her home where the rocks towered above her, abruptly protruding from the smooth sand. These boulders stood tall and erect in a "U" shape, creating what she considered a perfect temple by the ocean.

It was the place where her solitary chaise-shaped bench rested, facing the southeast so she could see and feel the sun rise, and if she sat at one end she could stretch out her legs and view the ocean. Here she would rest before making the trek back up the rock stairs that snaked their way up the thirty or so feet back to her home.

Now, with her run finished, she sat on her bench and took a hearty drink from the water bottle she habitually filled and placed on her bench before heading out.

Today she turned fifty-five. Her birthday—that hallmark

day that made everyone a year older. Yesterday she was fifty-four. Now that age was in the past forever, the same as every age before that.

She sighed. Another number, just another day. She closed her eyes and put her head back to feel the sun. If she opened her eyes, she could see the empty neighbouring beach home some distance away, but she kept them closed, shutting out everything except the sound of the pounding surf and the familiar comforting cry of the seagulls.

The crashing waves soon became the focus; over and over they rolled, forever in unceasing motion. She could feel the power within the constant pounding. She could feel it in every fibre of her being until she herself became the fluid motion of the water rolling in and out, her breath matching each wave and her body welcoming its calming motion.

Each day she would sit like this and wait. Wait for the thoughts and ideas. Today she didn't have to wait long.

Do something different today. It was insistent, this thought that popped into her head. *It's your birthday and you deserve a day off*.

"What am I to do?" she asked herself. The question prompted a similar conversation she'd had with her mother when she turned ten.

"My cherie! You are double digit today!" Her mother's amber eyes danced with delight. "The big one-oh!"

Andee did a pirouette in front of her mother.

"Do I look any older or different?" Amber eyes looked into amber eyes. Mother and daughter could have been twins had they been born the same year.

Anyone who ever saw Andee swore she was her mother

Amurlea all over again. Andee loved to hear that, for she thought her mother as a beautiful queen.

Amurlea shook her head. "Only more lovely, my little princess! Now, what would you like to do for your special birthday today, Andee? I have enough money for you and any friend you want for an evening out. Dinner and a movie. I promise…" Amurlea crossed her heart. "That I will drop you off and wait in the car at a discreet distance and won't interfere with your girls' night out."

As long as Andee could remember it was always just her and her mother. Her father was never a part of her life. Her mother had told her early on that her father died young and never got to know his child, and that she would not mourn his absence but be so very grateful to him because he gave her Andee. "We are you and me," she always said proudly, followed with a hug. There may have been a shortage of money in Amurlea's household, but there was always an abundance of love. So much so that Andee never felt shortchanged without a father.

Andee remembered answering that she wanted her best friend in the whole world to go with her.

"Well, we will have to ring Jasmine to see if she can go then," Amurlea stated matter-of-factly, for Andee and Jasmine were almost joined at the hip.

"No, not Jasmine," Andee said. "I want just you and me. Like it always is. And I want my cake to be my favourite oatmeal raisin cookies."

"Andee, are you sure?"

Andee nodded. "But we will have to get those numbered candles 'cause the other ones won't stick in a cookie."

Andee giggled as her mom scooped her up in a heartwarming embrace.

A slow, sad smile spread across Andee's face as she remembered her mother all those years ago. The conversation was just an echo in her memory.

She opened her eyes and looked down at the bench near where she sat. A small, brilliantly coloured bug with shiny greens and pearly blues perched itself beside her in its search for food and then scurried around in random directions.

"Well, hello there. Is it your birthday too? What do you think? Oatmeal cookies today? Not you? Ah, well, I think I'm going to bake myself some cookies and get a couple of those candles too." The bug opened it's wings and suddenly took flight. "Not your favourite, I see. I guess it is a little strange as a birthday cake, but what the heck, I never have followed the same drumbeat as others." She laughed a little. Talking to a bug only reinforced the loneliness she felt this day.

Andee stood to head back to the house and realized that today there would be no work for her, as she didn't feel inspired to do anything except bake those cookies.

Back at the house, Andee showered, dressed, and got herself ready for a trip into town. She had already searched the cupboards to see what was needed to bake her cookies.

Generally, her housekeeper, Carlita, who came in a couple of days a week, looked after all the grocery shopping and cooking, but she wasn't in today so Andee would have to pick up what she needed.

She sighed. Birthdays weren't her thing, and she didn't make a fuss over them. Today, though, she would do something different and make her own private celebration. Not everyone got to this age, so she decided she would celebrate that if nothing else.

She debated doing her hair and putting on a little makeup to brighten her amber eyes but decided that nothing was going to change how she felt. Her hair was fine in a ponytail and eyes would stay unadorned by makeup.

It wasn't until she backed her little Fiat out of her garage and pulled around to drive out of her driveway that she caught her reflection in the rear-view mirror. Some might still call her striking, but all she thought was *wow, the gray is really becoming prevalent*. She could feel another sigh begging for release as she remembered her hair was once a deep chestnut brown. *Was her hair really this gray? Or did it appear that way because she was a year older?* Out of habit, she brought her hands up to smooth any loose strands that had escaped the confines of her habitual style. She quickly realized this round of internal questions wasn't helping her to feel better and she chastised herself. *Don't look at yourself and it won't matter.*

Re-gripping the steering wheel, she focussed her attention to her hands, and she noticed the fullness they once had was no longer. *Maybe I should just stay home*, she thought and sat there, momentarily indecisive.

"Screw it," she spoke out loud. "Just go get the shit you need for the damn cookies, Andee." She berated herself. "Why does it always have to be such a production for you to skip routine? Today is your 'do something different' day. So just get on with it, will you?"

Checking the roadway for oncoming traffic, she pulled out before she changed her mind. Within a few minutes she was cruising past the empty rental house when she noticed a car parked in the driveway. It was a sleek, black, sporty, expensive, midlife-crisis-type of male-ego vehicle. She snorted as she drove past, imagining the owner. He would be in his fifties with a trophy wife who would be blonde, lithe, manicured, and young.

Andee spotted a man and women emerge from the door to head to the car. *You nailed it,* she thought. He was tall, handsome, and roughly her age. She was blonde, well dressed, beautiful, and young. *Of course,* she thought, *you know people.*

As quickly as the couple entered her thoughts they were forgotten as she made her way to town.

Kevin emerged from his newly acquired rental home. He could smell the salt from the ocean in the air. Such a calming effect. He looked over at Beverly who seemed intent to get the unpleasant task of setting foot in a grocery store over with as quick as possible. He raised his eyebrows at her apparent distaste of doing something so basic.

"Didn't you hire someone to do this?" There a hint of petulance in her voice.

"Yes, but it isn't settled yet and it may take a couple of days before she starts. So if we want to eat we need to buy groceries." He explained as patiently as he could.

"I just don't see why can't we eat out till she starts?"

Kevin looked over at Beverly as he started the car. While he enjoyed an occasional dinner out he preferred home cooked for everyday meals. Plus found he was good at it. Grocery shopping was all part of it.

He decided to take he would ignore Beverly's mood and make the most of their trip into town. The scenery before them was enough to spark his appreciation of the landscape and keep his mood light as they drove along the winding road.

Within fifteen minutes Andee arrived in the small town of Mendocino and was pulling up to the grocery store. Her little Fiat quickly and efficiently pulled into the closest parking spot.

The smiling store manager greeted her warmly when she entered. "Hello, Andee! What brings you into town?"

"Oatmeal and raisins, Bob! You got any?" She laughed as he approached her and gave her a warm pat on her shoulders. He was close to ten years older than she was and was the one who hired her when she moved here permanently ten years before. She was never so grateful to anyone as she was to Bob, who helped her she needed it.

"Well, my dear, you came to the right place." He laughed. "Down the same aisle it's always been. Not much changes around here!"

"I knew you wouldn't disappoint!" She gave him a fond smile as he moved on to his task at hand. He was always busy but never missed the opportunity to greet her.

Andee found what she needed without issue. As she was wheeling her cart to the checkout, a man and women hastily came around the corner.

Andee backed up, pulling her cart with her to avoid a collision, only to find that she stepped back too far into a cracker display. The boxes tumbled behind her in a crash that was audible throughout the store.

Embarrassed, she spun around to try to gather them all up again. The man quickly bent down to help Andee while muttering an apology.

"I'm so sorry, we were rushing around the corner too fast." The amber eyes that met Kevin's did not go unnoticed.

Andee looked up to see that it was Mr. Midlife Crisis and his wife. It was apparent to Andee that it was the missus who was navigating the cart, and yet she uttered no apology. In fact, she appeared to be impatient with her husband's efforts that delayed their own progress. She looked uncomfortable and out of place at the grocery store.

Bob had also heard the crash and came rushing from around the corner offering his apologies to Andee.

"Oh, Andee, leave that with me and we will get this sorted out. So very sorry. I guess it wasn't the best place for a display. I am sure you have more important things to be doing." He smiled a big warm smile in Andee's direction. Then with barely a glance at the man and woman, he began gathering up the boxes, placing them in an empty nearby cart. "I've got this."

The woman gave her husband a pouty look and spoke with a slight whine to her voice. "Kevin, leave that." She waved a hand in dismissal. "Let's go, we have such a busy day and we have to get back." She waited for a response from anyone. Having received none, she turned and left with Kevin, her high heels clicking on the polished surface. Her red-tipped fingers barely touched what she probably considered the germ-laden handle of the shopping cart.

Kevin looked at Andee apologetically and felt some embarrassment that he had no choice but to follow his partner's lead. Looking back over his shoulder at Andee he mouthed "I'm sorry."

Andee nodded and looked at the departing figures and shrugged before turning to finish her shopping. She almost forgot those candles.

CHAPTER
2

⁓

Back at the house, Andee dove into the process of building the recipe she had etched in her mind. Every measurement of every ingredient sparked memory on top of memory.

At times her eyes would fill up and she would chastise herself mentally, willing herself away from the melancholy that threatened to take hold.

Soon the freshly baked scent of her oatmeal raisin cookies filled the room. Putting her wares on the cooling rack, she paused to check her phone. Several messages had been left on it, all of them from the CC Jabber Agency. Carl and Carol Jabberly. Andee smiled at the number of calls made. It would be Carol, of course, wanting to wish her a happy birthday. Leaving a message would never do. If she had to call a dozen times, she would. Andee was sure it was Carol's tenacity that made the agency such a success; she never gave up.

Andee habitually teased them both about their names, Carol having one extra vowel than Carl's. It was appropriate that Carol had the "O," as the word "oh" was a mainstay in much of Carol's exuberance. "Oh my gosh," she would gush, or "oh, really?" or "oh boy." Or this was one of Andees' favourites: "Oh, you really have to hear this!" Andee loved them both and considered them family—the only family she had now, and they were both across the country in New York.

She looked at her watch. It was already past six. How long she had sat reminiscing she had no idea. Today time didn't seem to matter much to her. She would call them back in a little while.

Setting a cookie on a plate, she moved to the table, where her two number-five candles waited for the celebration. She re-arranged them so they sat just on the far side of her plate and lit them with a lighter.

For a while she sat there and watched them burn. She could once again hear her mothers' voice singing her "Happy Birthday."

Happy birthday to you...The memory echoed with the distance of years past. Then joining her mothers' voice was that of a young child. So many memories. Along with the notes that swirled in her mind, she could hear the clock ticking. Tick. Tick. Tick. Advancing time, moving further and further away from those happier times. *Happy Birthday to you*. Tick, tick.

She became acutely aware that the tap was dripping in the kitchen. Drip, drip, along with the tick, tick. The silence was deafening. To drown it out, she joined the birthday melody that chorused in her mind by singing it out loud.

"Happy birthday, dear Andee..." She blew out the candles. Rocking back and forth, the tears streamed down her cheeks and she willed herself to finish singing. "Happy ... birth ...

day to … you." The last words were just barely audible.

She noticed her phone light up again along with a familiar buzz and knew she had better pick it up, as Carol would call every hour on the hour till she did.

"Carol, hello." Andee managed to get the words out, trying to sound as though everything was okay and that she was glad to hear from her.

"Andee! You home? I tried calling you a few times. Why do you leave your cell phone at home when you're out? It's so difficult to get hold of you sometimes! Tell me you were out celebrating?" Without waiting for an answer, Carol rushed on. "Hey, happy birthday! The big five-five. Do you know what five and five symbolize?" Carol was into numerology. "I looked it up for you." She sounded as though she needed to take a breath but didn't.

Andee started to giggle. Leave it to Carol to unwittingly brighten her day without even realizing it.

"This number represents opportunities! Big time. It means transition and growth. A big year for you, Andee! It indicates life change. A welcome change, at that. Embrace change. That is very important. Hey, no laughing." Carol caught Andee's laughter. "Listen, Andee, if you want to start over, this is your year to do so and we have some very big news for you. VERY big. Hold on. Let me get Carl for you. Carl! Carl! I've finally got Andee! Carl! Can you hear me?" Andee could visualize all the hand gestures, and she wasn't surprised that even though Carol was using a cell phone she was hollering out to Carl. They were quite the couple. "Amusing" would best describe them, but also "madly in love" after decades together. "Oh, Andee, he is here now. I am going to put this on speaker. Carl!

Carl, come here. Andee. It's Andee on at the other end. Oh, Andee, here he is. I've put it on speaker. Can you hear us okay?"

Andee smiled. "Yes, Carol, I hear you fine." She could hear some bustling in the background and could envision Carl entering the room as he called out to her.

"Andee!"

"I'm here, Carl. How are you doing?"

"I'm doing great, Andee, as usual. Happy birthday!"

"Well, thank you."

"Hope you've been out celebrating. Carol has called endlessly according to what she tells me." He laughed heartily at his wife's exaggeration.

"Oh, Carl. Would you just tell her already, will you?" Carol sounded impatient to get her news out.

"What do you have, Carl? I am guessing that the book is doing okay?"

"Oh yes, my dear, it is about the book. You did it, Andee. All your books have been successful, but you knocked this one right out of the park. What can I say? Your first week out with Penny Forest and the book has hit The New York Times #1 bestselling book already and Andee, Paramount has called. They want the movie rights." Carl paused to take a deep breath. "And now we have to get moving on the book tour. We have it starting in two weeks and we have these guys from Paramount wanting to get together next week. Top brass, their lawyers and ours. We are going to get a deal rolling on this, girl. Next Thursday here in New York. I am assuming you can get out here Monday or Tuesday. Gives us time to read over the initial crack at a contract and review it with our lawyers. Look, I know it's short notice but they are also looking at all your

.

other books. This is huge, my girl."

"Wow." Andee was shocked. This was her tenth book and she felt it would do well but to have it viewed as a potential movie never crossed her mind.

"Can you get here by end of this week?"

"Yes." Andee nodded.

"Good. We will arrange your flight for Friday so we'll have some time to visit before we have to get down to business. Listen, Andee, we are so proud of you."

"Oh yes!" Carol chimed in. "Yes, and Andee, we love you! Looking so forward to our visit once you fly in. We will be there at the airport to pick you up. Now, the tour is going to cover four weeks and twenty stops, all in New York. It's going to be hectic, but I think we have it scheduled out so you can still get some down time."

"Okay." Four weeks once a year she could handle. Longer than that was too much.

"Well, my dear," Carl broke in. "We will have to wait to celebrate that, but today is your birthday. Hopefully you celebrated."

"Yes." Andee looked at her half-eaten cookie and burned candles. "Yes, I was in town with friends." She pictured the store manager and her new neighbours that she almost crashed into so she didn't feel like she was lying.

"Good!" Carl boomed. "Hopefully you got some cake and candles!"

Andee continued to look at the cookie and candles. "Yes, my favourite."

"Well, Andee, we are going to let you go, as it is late here and we have a big day tomorrow. Have a good night, girl, and all our best," Carl said.

"Yes, Andee, we will talk to you soon," Carol added. "Take care, love, and remember—big changes! This is only the start!"

"Talk to you both at the end of the week … and thank you both so much for the call and great news— and on my birthday, no less! Have a wonderful night!" As Andee ended the call she wondered about her internal reaction to the news. Hollow was the summation of it. She had all the material things and success she never even thought possible, and yet all she could feel was empty.

"Yes, Andee girl," she spoke out loud to herself. "Happy birthday to you."

CHAPTER

3

⟨⟨≈≫⟩

Andee woke up feeling renewed. The melancholy of her solitary birthday had moved on. She thought about how fortunate she was to have Carl and Carol in her life, and she quietly thanked her ex-husband for that relationship. It was through him that she met them at a banquet long before she enlisted them to become her literary agents. Without them, the opportunities she currently had in her life would simply not exist, and she knew that. She closed her eyes momentarily to let herself feel how fortunate she was.

She dressed in her running gear and hastily tied her hair back in the usual ponytail. The amber eyes that produced those lonely tears yesterday had a glimmer of a spark again. This whole movie thing now felt exciting. What would be involved? When she thought about it, her stomach fluttered. This was unknown territory that both excited and terrified her. Running would ground her again; this she knew without a doubt.

On the way out, she filled her bottle of water to drop off at her bench on the beach before her run.

The air was fresh, and she breathed it in deeply, savouring each breath. The sun was not yet cresting, but daylight had begun. She did this purposely so she would get the full experience of each and every sunrise she could. She could see that the colours had just started forming in the beauty of the gold, white, and pink spheres that dazzled the sky, which never failed to take her breath away. In rare moments like this, she revelled in being alive and for a moment forgot that she could ever feel alone.

Off she ran along the coast, her breath matching her exertion. Once again, she was lost in the rhythm of her movements. She ran with awe at everything she felt and saw in that moment.

On and on she went until it was time to turn back. Now she could feel the sun's warm rays as they caressed her arms, legs, and face. Her sweating body welcomed a slight breeze from the ocean until finally she could see her bench. The running finished, she slowed to a cool-down walk to her oasis.

Her routine was simple. She would sit on the bench, have a good long drink of water and sit quietly for a half hour, closing her eyes and breathing in the smell of the ocean. Listen to the waves crashing in, over and over.

"Hello." A male voice rudely interrupted her quiet reverie.

Andee's eyes flew open. Annoyance at the sudden jolt of awareness of another presence immediately rose within her, smashing her feelings of calm.

She easily recognized him from the grocery-store incident.

"Allow me to introduce myself. Kevin Coultier." He held his

hand out in greeting. "I think we met yesterday. Did we not?"

Andee put her hand just above her eyes to shield them from the sun, deliberately ignoring his outstretched hand. She had already formed an opinion of him from his flashy car and the grocery store. Not that she had found him rude, but his wife was, and she considered that an extension of him. She had subconsciously chosen a lesser view of her new neighbours with the intent to never get to know them, and now here he was.

He stood directly in front of the sun mounting on the horizon. This created an intense array of light all around him, which effectively erased all details of the man into a shadowy form. All she could see was this darkened outline in the brilliance of the colour show.

Kevin's hand dropped to his side.

"I, ah, thought to introduce myself, as we are neighbours now." He pointed to the once-empty house on the beachfront a good walking distance from Andee's home. He wondered if he imagined the blatant rudeness that appeared obvious from this woman whom he had met only once.

"I see," was all the response she provided. People came, people went. It was a vacation rental house, after all. No point in really getting to know each new neighbour. Usually after the first introduction she wouldn't see them and after a few weeks they went back to wherever they came. Simple as that. She had no interest in this introduction, either.

"You never know when you might need your neighbour, I always say." He was rambling, he knew, but never had he been greeted so coolly. Well, "frozen" might be a better term. Women usually purred with welcome when he flashed his smile.

"You must be Andee. I've spoken with Carlita Sanchez." Carlita worked for Andee two days a week, but she also was hired by the owner of the rental home to look after keeping it clean, overseeing that the groundskeeper did his part as well as ensuring that any damages were noted when the holiday tenants' left. She took her jobs most seriously. "And I was hoping to run into you." He laughed at the pun, as he was just heading out for his morning run.

Great, Andee thought. Is this what she was going to have to deal with every morning during the course of his stay?

"She tells me that she works at your place Tuesdays and Thursdays. I'd like to hire her for a couple of the days she has off, if that is okay with you." Kevin was finding this conversation was becoming more difficult with each passing word he uttered. He was trying to be polite but found Andee to be lacking in that department.

Andee looked up at him from where she sat. He was no longer standing in front of the sun and she could see him better. He was tall and athletic with a dazzling smile that she was sure was a winner with the ladies.

"Carlita is the one you should be asking. Her time is her own, as she chose the days that she comes to my house. If she chooses to work for you, it has nothing to do with me."

Kevin nodded. "Well … I see." He was about to say it was a pleasure to meet her but couldn't. Instead, he mumbled that he had to be on his way and carried on. Starting with a slow jog, he moved away from the woman he just met. His thoughts briefly lingered on those very striking amber eyes that exuded intellect and impatience. Of course, there was that lithe little figure that radiated a strength and grace that belied what he guessed her age to be. He estimated she would be close to his age if not a little younger, as it did not escape him that her hair boasted many gray strands and fine lines had formed around her eyes. Oddly enough, this combination only produced a show of wisdom versus aging. The physical qualities, however fine they were, were not the predominate impression that was left with him. Her rudeness was. With a wry grin, he thought of the realtor who had mentioned how wonderful the neighbours were and that he would find them welcoming and friendly. Obviously he had never met Andee.

Andee sat there a moment longer, knowing that her mother would have been shocked at her discourtesy, and yet could not shake the annoyance she felt without knowing why. She was also aware that she had labelled him with less than desirable qualities before she even met him. She knew it wasn't fair and that she was using this intrusion to reinforce her annoyance. *What has gotten into you?* she berated herself before deciding that her quiet reverie was not to be that day. She got up and left.

In two days she would be heading east, and she had much to do before then. Mentally making a list, she headed back up the curving rock stairway to her home. Each stone was carefully placed to make the climb easier, yet despite how much running she did she was still breathless by the time she reached the top.

At the top she always paused to catch her breath and would turn back toward the ocean. Its beauty never escaped her, and gratitude would flood her every time she hiked those stairs … this place she loved so well.

By the time she reached the house, Carlita was there.

"Morning, Miss Andee, I see that you met Mr. Kevin."

Andee smiled at Carlita. No matter how many times Andee told her to drop the "miss," Carlita just couldn't bring herself to do so. She was old school and felt it was a show of respect for her employer. "I told him to speak to you about my doing extra time at the rental."

Andee gave a wave of her hand in a "that wasn't necessary" gesture. "Carlita, I told him your time is your own and that you will be the one who decides. Besides, they never stay there long anyway."

Carlita busied herself in the kitchen. On Tuesdays she would cook and do some baking plus odd chores. On Thursdays she did a thorough cleaning. This time around she was only to cook for the next couple of days. She cleared out the fridge, pulling out any food that would spoil while Andee was away and setting it on the counter.

"Not this one," she stated. Her dark brown eyes scanned the food set before her, deciding what type of a meal she could make from it. Hands on her ample hips, she glanced at Andee to see her eyebrows raised in question.

"You mean they bought the place?"

"No, leasing it. For two years." Carlita nodded, emphasizing her statement while also affirming her decision as to what she wanted to make. "How about a casserole with this? I will freeze what you don't eat before you leave. That way you will have something to eat when you get back. But I will also have the fridge ready with fresh produce, juice, and your coconut milk."

Andee nodded. No matter what Carlita made she always enjoyed it.

"Two years?" She felt dismay when she thought of her quiet-time interruption this morning.

"Yes, ma'am." Carlita pulled out the cutting board and a knife. Chopping expertly, she continued to speak. "He owns the engineering firm that designed the new hotel that is going up in town. Big one. Apparently they are starting to move dirt next week. Says he'll be here off and on over the course of the build. The first year is very important. So he says." She shrugged as though it didn't matter to her how much time he spent there. The knife cleanly and efficiently finished up the round of vegetables. Dropping them in a mixing bowl, she pulled out some seasoning and a can of tomatoes.

Andee put some bread in the toaster, working around Carlita as she spoke, thinking *god forbid he feels obligated to stop each morning to say hello and produce idle chatter.* She really hoped he was going to be too busy to bother with her. Well, if he did try to talk to her, she would have none of it. In fact, she was quite relieved that she reacted to him as she did this morning.

The following morning was a repeat of Tuesday morning, with Kevin politely stopping to say good morning and working very hard for some small talk. Andee repeated her chilly performance and found she had to do the same for Thursday. Really, he was slow to get her hints. She was beginning to worry that an abrupt "get off my beach" statement would have to be made before it would sink in for him. It was so typical of his type. He couldn't understand that his charm wasn't required or wanted.

Carlita came in on Thursday morning and made a comment about "Mr. Kevin" and how he found "Miss Andee" a prickly pear.

Andee could only roll her eyes. If he found her so prickly, then why didn't he take the hint and leave her be? Not that it would matter, for in less than twenty-four hours she would be heading east again for a month.

PART II

Listen to your calling,
That little voice within.
Speaking, guiding, internal.
Its' magic song will sing.
The clues are there.
Quietly waiting.
With only one thing left to do,
Follow.
Follow all the way through.

The path.

CHAPTER
4

Friday morning brought with it a much-needed rain, which happened so rarely out here. *How apt,* Andee thought as she got ready to leave. The weather mirrored how she always felt when she left this place. But then again, maybe it was time for a break away. Heading out the door, she made sure everything was locked, and without a look back she drove out the driveway and made her way to the airport.

Andee was a true believer of living life in the most comfortable way she could. Keep it simple. The "stuff" and "privileges" that money could bring really meant very little to her. There was no one she tried to impress, least of all herself. This was one of the reasons she drove a Fiat and flew economy. It wasn't to save money, for she had enough. She was just like everyone else and could see no value in trying to separate herself from who she really was. It was what she always did before, and she saw no need to change. Besides, she would often get some of her best inspirations for her novels from the people she met briefly as a passenger.

Today would be no different. She read her seat number and found herself near the back of the plane in a middle seat. After stuffing her carry-on in the overhead, she settled herself in to prepare for the long flight. Comfortable in jeans, a t-shirt, and sneakers, she stretched out her legs.

Within a few moments a young woman with long blonde hair and startling blue eyes smiled at Andee. With an apologetic gesture she indicated that she had the window seat, forcing Andee back out to the aisle while the girl slid in.

"No problem," Andee returned the smile. They were going to be sitting side by side for over four hours, so Andee figured she might as well introduce herself. The girl informed Andee that her name was Shelly. Andee guessed her to be in her mid-twenties. She had been on a retreat in California and was heading back home to New York.

They made chit-chat for the first hour then Andee settled in for a nap while Shelly watched a movie. Andee wasn't sure how long she had been sleeping when she woke up in time for a snack. It was then that she noticed Shelly had some playing cards out. Upon further inspection she realized they weren't regular cards.

"What are those?"

"Well, these are Tarot cards," Shelly explained.

"Oh." Andee had heard of Tarot readers but had no experience with them. She was about to leave it be but decided to ask what they did.

"They are used for readings for people who just want clarification in their lives. Each card has a basic meaning, yet they are full of symbols and colours, which all have meaning, and also each one is numbered, which can have meaning. All of these create the reading or story for a person with questions."

"I have a friend who is big into numerology. So it is similar to that?"

"Well, yes and no. But I guess you could say yes." Shelly paused. "No matter what is used, it's a tool, and that is really what the cards are. It all works the same anyway."

Andee raised her eyebrows questioningly, which prompted Shelly to continue.

"The higher self directs the person with the question while they shuffle the deck, making them stop at the appropriate time. The reader taps into their energy so that the proper signs, symbols, feelings, whether they be physical or emotional, are made known to the reader," Shelly explained.

It all sounded a little farfetched for Andee to believe.

"Would you like me to do a reading for you? I usually charge, but I will give this one as a gift. Maybe you could use a gift?" She shrugged in a small gesture as though it mattered not to her whether Andee accepted her offer or not.

"Well … okay," Andee accepted. "What do I do?"

"Alright." Shelly became very professional. "Take a few slow, deep breaths to relax while I ask for the highest good to come through for you."

Humouring Shelly as best she could, Andee took a few deep breaths and exhaled slowly. Shelly closed her eyes and whispered something to herself, after which she waved her hands over the deck.

Andee was curious. "What did you just do?"

Shelly focussed on the deck while she moved her hands over it again. "I am clearing any energies left over from previous readings." She was quite matter-of-fact about the process.

"Okay, now…" She handed the deck over to Andee. "I want you to shuffle. No talking or comments. I just want you to focus putting your energy into the cards as you shuffle. Picture energy or love moving from your heart, down your arms, into your hands, and they in turn will move that from your fingers into the deck. Continue to shuffle until you think you have done enough. Then stop."

Andee began to shuffle, doing exactly as instructed. She could feel her heart pounding in her chest. Thinking of her pulsing blood as her energy, she moved it from her heart and out through her arms as she shuffled. Carefully, she focussed on the energy moving forward to the hands, fingers, and finally the deck. She could feel it literally move with each thump. She was very conscious of it until finally she felt she had done enough.

Shelly had her split the deck once with her left hand, then again. Finally, she instructed Andee to stack it from right to left. Carefully, she took the deck from Andee.

Using the seat tray in front of her, Shelly placed one card down. It was a dark card showing a tower against a black background, with a bolt of lightning fiercely striking the tower, lighting it ablaze. The force of the lightning strike ripped the top of the tower off its peak, which created a devastating crack right down to its very foundation, making it precariously dangerous. The windows had people leaping from them in fear to escape the fiery inferno and the potential collapse of the building. At the same time it appeared that those who jumped for their safety ultimately jumped to their own demise.

"This is the Blasted Tower. A card of sudden change. A

clearing of old, outworn ways. Yours." Shelly looked directly at Andee, her startling blue eyes seeming to pierce right through her as though she could see everything. Andee's heart pounded in her chest so vehemently she could hear its roar in her ears. For a moment she could hear nothing else, and then Shelly's voice pierced through to her conscious. "It literally symbolizes that everything you know and the walls you have built up so carefully around you will tumble. This wall of self-protection only succeeded in holding you back." She shook her head. "You will feel as though it is crumbling around you, but there is a glimmer of hope and opportunity. One very small action with huge ramifications. You will be the one who decides whether it will be positive or otherwise. You are a very powerful woman, and this will become clear to you even if it does not make sense now, but I am hoping that some of it will. Does it?"

Andee nodded. There was some truth to her words. She couldn't help but think of Carol's prediction of the double fives—her book and the movie deal.

Shelly pulled out another card and laid it across the Blasted Tower. It depicted a solitary woman amidst what appeared to be a flourishing garden. She was elegantly dressed in finery while one arm with a gloved hand was carefully extended. Perched on the gloved hand sat a falcon. The woman seemed perfectly at ease as she faced her bird of prey. Along each side of her flowing gown, nine large coins seemed to float up from the lavish garden.

"This is the Nine of Pentacles. She represents an independent woman. She is the challenge for this change to happen. This woman is you. This is an indicator that you must be open to others."

Another card was drawn and set to the left of the first two cards. It depicted a heart set against a dark, gray, stormy, rain-filled sky with three daggers plunged right through it; one down the centre and the other two on either side of the centre. It was not a pleasant-looking card.

"This is the Three of Swords, and it is a card that is the past leading to the current. I feel the heart break from multiple events, one that sealed the fate of another. Know that this is the past, and although you will carry the scars, you will move beyond it. The timing is now right. It has been a long journey. But again, you must not block the chance to change."

Another card was pulled from the top of the deck. It was the Death card. Andee wanted Shelly to stop, but somehow she couldn't ask. Emotions were whirling. Spinning. Making her stomach tie itself in knots. How could Shelly know and see this? She felt like she was holding her breath but couldn't let it out.

"This is the Death card, and it is a very good card to receive in this position. It is the conclusion to the Blasted Tower. This Death card is also a card of change, one that indicates a gradual change from your past." Shelly pointed to the pierced heart. "You didn't see these coming, but this…"—she pointed to the Death card— "this will help you move on gradually. Again, a clearing of the old, outworn ways and unhealthy habits. Yes, this is very positive. Four to eight months, I'd say."

She lay out the next card. This depicted a man with a staff in one hand and the world in another hand. Behind him stood yet another staff. "This is the Two of Wands. It is a choice of where you place your energy. You have the courage to do this now. It may be time to share with someone what is very deep within you. This is what is in your resources. What you will tap into to move forward."

Another card was drawn. "This is your aim." She placed this above the Blasted Tower.

Andee wondered how many cards would be drawn, as they had very little room to put out any more. This card was very pleasing. It showed a nude man and woman facing each other with an angel peering down upon them. The angel was cast in front of a very brilliant sun and its wings fluttered above the couple while its arms were outstretched almost as though it were to ready to swoop down to embrace them. For some reason she thought of Kevin as he stood in front of the sun the other morning.

"The Lovers card." Shelly had a slight smile. "It is a card of coming together, forming a true partnership, if you may. You are truly a loving person. Ah, yes, but that has been blocked for a long time." With this, she looked directly into Andee's eyes again. "You are very aware of what power love is and you need to apply it to areas lacking. For yourself. If you can do this, amazing things will happen for you."

Andee stared at Shelly. Her words, all of them, struck an emotional cord within her and she found that she was very close to tears. She was not able to speak.

Shelly placed yet another card. "The Hanged Man. See things from a different perspective, otherwise you will continue to be caught in a state of limbo. I am not speaking of material possessions, as you have abundance there." She tapped the card with the woman and falcon and then looked back at the heart. "But of the heart. Neither moving forward and unable to move back, no matter how much you want to."

She tapped the Two of Wands. "Make your choice wisely."

The eighth card was drawn. "The Queen of Wands. This is how others see you. Powerful, independent, in control. You are a wise woman. Do what feels right for you, as your heart knows best."

The ninth card was pulled from the deck. It was a man and woman again facing each other, each holding a chalice. This couple was fully clothed, and the man appeared to be reaching for the woman. A winged lion head hovered just above, looking down on them while holding a rod from which two snakes were coiled, creating the symbol for health.

"This is your hopes and fears." Tapping the card with her finger, Shelly looked up at Andee again. "Do not fool yourself that you are happy on your own."

"This is the last card that I will draw for you." Shelly turned over the card she spoke of. "The Ten of Pentacles. A completion or coming together. A reunion of sorts." She frowned. "A man and woman. Although this card shows an older man, I see it as a woman."

This card showed an elderly man looking on another couple that was dancing in celebration. "This younger woman. You see?"

Andee nodded.

"It's you, and there is the shadow of a boy. He is in the background with you. He is the instrument in building this family." Once again, Shelly looked directly into Andee's eyes. "Your family."

Looking back down at the card, Shelly stated. "I need to pull one more. Sorry. Usually I stop at ten, but there is another." She did not see that a tear sprang forth in Andee's eye that made its way down her cheek.

"Hmm. Another ten. The Ten of Cups. Emotional completion. A complete family. Partner, son, and daughter. You will feel complete. Whole." She held a hand open and then pulled her fingers together as she emphasized her words. "Eleven months, a year."

Andee shook her head, tears rolling down unabashedly. "Please … no more."

Shelly looked at Andee and appeared horrified that she upset her. "Okay, I am so very sorry. I didn't mean to upset you. This is a beautiful reading. Full of love." She put a hand on Andee's arm in a comforting gesture before withdrawing it to pick up her cards. Tucking them away in their case, she looked at Andee and again mouthed, "I'm sorry." She then reached into her bag to pull out a notebook and pencil. She began writing as fast as she could.

Andee paid no attention to Shelly as she tried to quell that internal calamity. Her thoughts were tumbling and crashing against one another. The reading was fairly accurate, except the family part. She had no family and no way she could start one now at her age. Never going to happen. That was sure. She did not have the heart to tell Shelly how wrong she was, so when Shelly handed her the pages of what she wrote out, she just took them, barely registering that Shelly was explaining it was a summary of what she read and saw. "For reviewing in the future, and here is my business card if you ever want another or know someone else who might be interested. I can do them online as well as in person."

Andee only muttered a quick thanks and placed the papers and card in her briefcase side pocket. Shortly thereafter, they began to prepare for landing and then departed the plane, each to go their own way. Andee would put this behind her as an interesting way to pass the time on a long flight across the country. She would make sure she forgot the jumbled array of painful emotions that had surfaced so unexpectedly and sliced her heart for that brief moment. She was alone, and there was nothing that would change that.

CHAPTER
5

Andee pulled her luggage off the carousal and quickly made her way out of the last of the airport checks. Once through, it didn't take her long to find Carl and Carol. A bear hug from Carl ensued with Carol joining in to make it the group hug that it always became. If there was an opportunity for embraces, Carol was in.

Catching up was more Carol filling Andee in on everything. Detailed to the core, she left nothing out as they made their way back to Carol and Carl's place.

"Tomorrow we take you back to your apartment, but tonight you are with us." Carol held up her hand that would bode with no arguments from Andee as Carl expertly weaved their way through traffic. It was closing in on dinner, and they had it ready. For Andee, it was more like late lunch and she was grateful, as it was some hours now since she had eaten anything.

"I hope you don't mind." Carol gave Andee an apologetic

look. "But I have taken the liberty of booking you a hair appointment for Monday morning." It was something Carol automatically did, for she was quite aware that Andee took very little time with her appearance.

"I know." Andee rolled her eyes, then proceeded to mimic Carol's voice and usual phrase. "We want to portray the classy style of a successful writer."

The women were laughing heartily as Carl quickly looked them both over. He knew it had to be said every year. Being stylish just wasn't at the top of Andee's to- do list.

"This time around I want to keep my gray. Maybe have some fun with platinum colour. I decided it's time to celebrate my age instead of fighting with it." Andee said.

Carol was thoughtful as she looked at Andee and then nodded in agreement. "Yes, I think that would really work well."

The weekend was spent catching up and doing some shopping. Andee loved New York whenever she was there but never really missed it when she left. Not like she felt when she left California behind; every morning when she rose she missed the coastline. The sights, smells, and sound of it. It was part of her; it was where she felt at home.

Monday morning came quickly, and Carol smiled with approval as she surveyed Andee after her appointment with the hairdresser. "Beautiful."

Andee's hair was cut in layers, but she made sure it was still long enough to tie back. It fell into a flattering, face-framing style that included wisps for bangs. The new streaks blended perfectly with the natural gray that was already there and gave Andee a mature and youthful look, if you could ever put those two words together in one sentence.

Back at the CC Jabber Agency offices they began to review her schedule and a copy of the preliminary contract that Paramount had forwarded. Andee was taken by surprise at what she considered a very generous offer to which Carl, Carol, and their lawyers agreed. Some changes in the verbiage was all they felt needed, and by Thursday everything was completed and the copies were signed. They would start work the following year on the movie, and Andee was thrilled to be included as a consultant.

The evening was spent in a celebratory dinner at a very posh restaurant and it was here that Andee decided to tell Carl and Carol what she had been thinking for a while now. "I need to tell you both something."

"Sure." Carl seemed relaxed and happy, probably because he was with his favourite girls and he felt like a king.

"I want to take a bit of a break from writing."

Both Carl and Carol looked surprised.

Carol was the first to recover. "This is a bit shocking, Andee."

"I know, but I need a break. Right now I am in a very good position financially to do that, and I think the timing is right. I don't want to disappoint anyone, but I really need this. I was thinking of taking a long trip. Maybe different places around the world. Africa, Australia, Ireland. Anywhere, really."

Carol raised an eyebrow while she continued to read her menu. Without looking up, she stated what was on her mind. "I don't believe you want to take time off to travel. Nothing was stopping you before, and I know you hate travelling."

Pausing deliberately, she set her menu down and peered at Andee over the top of her glasses. "So what is it?"

Andee sighed. "I don't know. I can't put a finger on it, but there is a restlessness that I'm feeling and I don't know what to do about it. Sometimes I get so frustrated with myself because I have had such a wonderful career with my writing and I know I should feel more grateful for it, and I try. However, I can't seem to shake that restlessness and I cannot pinpoint what it is. I just feel it. Also, right now I don't have anything else in the wings for another book. That hasn't happened before. Usually, the next one is popping in before the one I'm working on is finished."

"Darling, why don't you come back to New York then?" Carl squeezed her hand. "This was once your home. You really don't do anything in California except hole up in that house of yours. Maybe it's time to connect with people again."

"Carl, my home is in California. I miss it like crazy when I am not there."

"Maybe that's the problem, dear," Carol chimed in. "Maybe you need a change of scenery like Carl suggested? You are far too comfortable there by yourself. Shake it up a little. But in the meantime, I agree that it would be good for you to take some time off. That will give you ample opportunity to figure this out. Once you do then I am quite sure the creative spark will light you up again." The drinks were brought to the table just as Carol was finishing that last sentence. "In the meantime, we celebrate and get ready for those book tours."

Raising her glass, Carol toasted to all.

Tomorrow would be another day, and the tour would begin. As past experience proved, it would likely fly by.

Enjoy this, Andee, she thought, for it may be the last tour if another book idea didn't come along.

Andee sat in a chair behind the table that held copies of her book. The book tour felt as though it had just begun and was now winding down with this final stop. She surveyed the lineup of people who came to see her. So many different individuals. Not for the first time she found herself wondering if it would be the final tour she did.

It never escaped her the wonder she felt at all these people who took time out of their schedule to see her and tell her how much they enjoyed her books. Would they be disappointed in her if another didn't materialize?

They were mostly adults of all ages. She knew the books had a wide audience and that Penny Forest was a huge hit with her fans. They told her, each and every one that had waited in line to see her over these last number of weeks. She made it a point to thank all of them properly and give each one her undivided attention when they got to the front of the line. She tried to take in all the details of each one, as they made her feel worthwhile, only to be disappointed in herself as the more she met the more blended they became.

She studied the next woman in line. A dark-haired young beauty and mother to boot, if the toddler in her arms belonged to her. Andee didn't doubt that he did.

"This is your son?"

The woman nodded, seemingly thrilled that she made it to the front of the line.

"He's beautiful."

The woman beamed. "Thank you!" she gushed, and rushed on, "It is so nice to meet you, Ms. Pearce. I love your books. I have such a hard time putting them down once I start reading one." She looked at her son with a somewhat guilty look. "I have to put a timer on so I put it down when I should, otherwise my chores don't get done." She giggled a nervous little laugh and pulled out the book she just purchased. "Could you sign this for me, please? My name is Jen."

"Sure." Andee smiled. "Anything in particular?"

Jen shook her head. "Just whatever is fine."

"Okay." Andee wrote out *Dear Jen, Thank you from my heart. Your kind words remind me why I love to write. May life continue to bless you with all the best that it has to offer.*

Love Andee.

The woman gave Andee a bright smile before moving on. Next was an elderly gentleman who walked with a cane in one hand and held a book in another.

The first thing she noticed about him was his brilliant blue eyes that shone with intelligence and humour.

"Thank you so much for coming out. Would you like a seat?" Andee motioned that he should come around the table while she stood and offered her chair to him. He shook his head, stating he was fine, but Andee had already vacated her chair for him. The store staff proved to be very accommodating and quickly produced another chair before he could protest further.

"How are you this evening?" Andee smiled as they sat side by side.

"I am well," came his reply, along with an appreciative smile.

She took his hand. "I hope you weren't waiting too long."

He shook his head.

"Do you have family?" she asked.

"Yes, I have children and grandchildren."

"Did any of them come with you?"

"No." He shook his head. "I am on my own this evening. I came because I wanted to tell you how much I love and enjoy reading your books. Such magic and thrills. You have a brilliant imagination, and I thank you for sharing. I was wondering if I might trouble you to sign my book for my grown daughter who is also a fan. She lives out of state."

"Of course. What is her name?"

"Cherie."

Andee pulled the book open and wrote.

For Cherie,

All my thanks for your support.

May love and family be abundant in your life.

Love Andee

She smiled at the gentleman with the blue eyes.

As the evening wore on, she focussed on the beautiful smiles, warm handshakes, praise, and love she felt. Her heart was full, yet sad, as she wondered if she would ever meet them again.

The next day she would be back at the airport to fly home. She was looking forward to it—the cliffs, beach, and the pounding surf. But mostly she was looking forward to her quiet again.

She thought of her conversation with Carl and Carol over their celebratory dinner and wondered what was going to fill her day if she didn't write. Then as suddenly as she thought it, she knew it really wasn't something to worry about. That would look after itself. Whatever this restlessness was inside, it too would work itself out and there was really no need to worry or put effort into that either.

CHAPTER
6

True to Carlita's word she had the fridge stocked up so when Andee arrived home there was fresh fruit and vegetables along with the thawing casserole she made when Andee left.

"Bless her," Andee said aloud. Carlita was always one to anticipate what was needed.

It was evening and she could see that her neighbour's light was on. She found it somewhat comforting to know that she wasn't all alone. After having the activity of New York life it was an adjustment to come back to complete silence, even though she looked forward to it. *Funny we humans are,* she thought. *We want something and when we get it, we can quickly find the shortfalls of the very thing we desired.*

After her run tomorrow she knew she would be settled back into her routine. She wondered if it was her quiet time in the oasis that seemed to make everything make sense again. After a quick bite, she took her exhausted body up the stairs and literally fell into her bed. The familiar and comforting feel of it left her sinking deeply into the softness of her sheets and mattress. Her last thought before sleep engulfed her was she should probably change and brush her teeth.

The next morning dawned with its familiar habit of blazing glory while Andee revelled in it. All her senses were alive and bursting as she ran. It felt so good to move freely and to hear and smell all that she missed this past month. She breathed deeply and had to push herself to finish the complete run, as she found that the past month of little exercise indeed made its impact felt.

She arrived at her bench and drank her water. It was cool and refreshing and hit the spot. She could feel her sweat gathering in tiny rivulets that assembled themselves until gravity pulled and teased them like tiny bugs running between her breasts and down her body. She halted the progress, using her T-shirt to mop them up, adding to the dampness that already prevailed through the shirt.

Closing her eyes, she focussed on the sounds that surrounded her. It was a finely tuned orchestra, its symphony growing in intensity as she breathed in and out. The seagulls' cry added to the perfection of the crashing waves. Back and forth, breathe in, breathe out. She was home.

"Hello there!" A male voice ripped through her sweet homecoming. Instantly irritated, Andee scowled but kept her eyes closed.

"How are you?" he continued. "Haven't seen you for a while. You must've been away?"

She swore internally with vehement vulgarity before adding *damn it all, anyways. What was he doing here?*

She slowly opened her eyes. "Kevin. Ah, yes. Yes, I was away for a month. But now I am back and was looking forward to my peace and quiet." Her response was clipped.

"Ah yeah, I know exactly what you mean. I just love it here."

Andee was afraid of that.

"You know, it just rejuvenates me. I feel like I'm whole when I run out here."

"And I'm sure you should carry on with your rejuvenation. Good way to start your day, and I will carry on with my rest here. Alone. Like I always do. By myself. Quietly." She made sure to emphasize her last few sentences slowly.

"Yes, I should carry on, as I have a busy day. Nice seeing you again, Andee. Likely see you tomorrow if you are going to be around." He nodded. "Ah yes, a beautiful day. You have a great one!"

With that, Kevin turned to carry on with his run. He tried so hard to be nice to her, but found her to be an enigma. He couldn't see any harm in greeting her in the mornings and yet her response to him was always sharp. Whatever was behind her usual reaction to his greetings, he was sure time would provide the answers. In the interim, he would continue to treat her as a gentleman should.

"Shit." Now she swore out loud between her teeth but kept it under her breath in case he could still hear her. Her thoughts were rambling. *Not again. Damn it. Damn it all, anyway. How was she going to get through to him that she wanted her quiet? Alone. How much clearer could she make it?*

Her irritation ensued, and her shattered peaceful calm remained elusive. She tried desperately to restore it before she finally gave up and headed up to her house. Carlita would be there shortly, and she wanted to shower and start her breakfast. She knew Carlita would want to hear all about her trip.

By the time she was done her shower, her irritation had ebbed and she felt better. Just in time, because Carlita arrived when Andee entered the kitchen to start her breakfast.

Carlita swooped Andee up with a bear hug as soon as she came into the kitchen. "So tell me all about it, Miss Andee! How was New York?"

"Fabulous. Everything went so well, and I have some news!" Andee paused for emphasis, then clapped her hands. "I signed a contract for a movie deal!"

Carlita's jaw dropped in shock before the news sunk in. Then she literally bounced with excitement for Andee. "My goodness, Miss Andee! That is amazing news! Oh, my goodness!" For once she had no words and just grabbed her boss in another crushing hug.

"I know, amazing, isn't it? Come, sit for a while and have a coffee with me. I will tell you all about New York and my experiences." Andee motioned toward the table. They usually sat for an hour whenever she came back from her annual visit east, and Andee would tell Carlita about the city, shopping, people, food, lights, and the whole feeling. Whenever Andee spoke about New York, it was as though Carlita could feel and relive every moment; almost like she had been there herself. She would close her eyes and see the shops, feel the clothes, and see the price tags. She was sure the amazing descriptions were what made Andee the spectacular novelist she was. It was really no surprise that one of her novels would capture the interest of the movie world.

Once Andee was done spinning her tales of her travels, she

asked Carlita how things were there.

"No changes here." Carlita stood up to get back to work. "Everything ran smooth." She brought her left hand up to slide it gracefully outwards to indicate no bumps. "I am settling in well at Mr. Kevin's too. He has a good routine, and I know what he likes for food. He is not fussy on vegetables." She shook her head and waved a finger as though she were his mother. "But I do his shopping and cook them anyway and say he bought them and should eat what he bought."

Andee smirked and rolled her eyes while thinking he wouldn't win with Carlita. If she thought she was right she didn't give up.

"What does his wife think of you taking over the menu like that?' Andee took a sip of coffee. Her breakfast eaten, she was on her second cup. Carlita began clearing away the dishes to make room to do some cooking before she started the other housework. Both women had a good routine and loved talking with each other, but if Carlita came to work, she worked. She had developed the habit of working in the kitchen on the mornings she was there while Andee sipped coffee. That way they could have a short visit and Carlita could do what she came to do before Andee got working on her writing.

"Tish." Carlita waved a hand in dismissal before reaching under the sink for the dish rack and dish soap. "He is not married, nor is he living with anyone."

Andee was confused. "Well, who was that blonde woman I saw him with in town?'

Carlita rolled her eyes. "That was the one before the brunette that he has now. I wonder if a redhead is next." She was implying that as he hasn't settled down by now, it wasn't likely to happen and he had an array to pick from. She waved a motherly finger in the air as she continued. "He seems a nice man, so I don't know why he can't find himself a nice woman."

Andee had an immediate answer for that one, as she thought, *because he's an egotistical, woman-preying pain in the ass.* She was careful to keep it as a thought because she also knew Carlita well. The woman had a habit to be a bit of a gossip at times, even if she tried to be discreet about it. She also pretended it was her honourable duty to find out the truth whether it had anything to do with her or not.

Carlita looked at the clock. Andee usually would have moved along to her office by this time but she lingered at the table. "Don't you have something to work on?" Carlita asked bluntly.

"Nope." Andee grabbed an apple, took a good-size bite out of it and began chewing. "Taking some time off." It came out a little garbled with the mouthful of apple.

Carlita paused in mid swipe while wiping down a plate in a sink full of sudsy water. She gave Andee a sharp, questioning look but didn't say a word.

"I am tired and in need of a break." Andee finally swallowed the piece of apple.

"How will you fill in your day? Will you still need me if you have all this time on your hands?" Carlita looked as though she felt like her feet had slid out from under her.

"Don't you worry about that. I will figure something out and know that you are still needed here."

Carlita raised one eyebrow as if in doubt. Now she seemed concerned that her employer would be underfoot.

Andee was quick to reassure her. "And don't worry about

that either." She took another bite and slid off her chair. "In the meantime, I think I'll go to town for a while." She knew Carlita worked best alone without interruption.

Grabbing her bag, Andee headed out the door and towards her car with no idea about what to do other than go for a drive. Making her way along the familiar road she drove past Kevin's place and noted that his car was gone. Suddenly she was very curious about the hotel he was working on and found herself heading in that direction. She knew where it was going to be built on the east side of the town and found that much progress with dirt moving had been made while she had been away. As she slowly drove past, she spotted Kevin in deep conversation with another man, both wearing the required hard hat. She reluctantly had to admit that he was a very handsome man, and if she was going to be truthful, she also had to admit to a little bit of curiosity where he was concerned, although she could not say why.

She decided to head to the library, where she found a couple of fiction books and one on learning how to paint. *Hmm*. She thought about her ocean view and wondered if she could learn to paint it. After all, she had decided to take a break and what better way to improve on her creativity than to learn a new artistic endeavour? Happy that she had a new focus, at least for the time being, she left the library and flipped through the art book. Might as well see what type of supplies were needed before she left town. She spotted a picnic bench a short distance away in a tiny alcove tucked in between some of the storefronts.

There were several of these sitting areas where locals and tourists could rest during the heat of the day, as they provided some needed shade from a few trees and the buildings that surrounded them. The town also took pride in those tidy little spots and carefully adorned them with planters that contained vibrant flowering cacti. Pretty and quaint is how Andee would describe them. She sat on the bench and pulled out a piece of paper and pen from her purse. Flipping to the materials page, she began to write out her list.

"Andee!" She looked up and saw Kevin crossing the street towards her. *Seriously?* She felt like her face likely had an expression bordering on rudeness.

"Oh, Kevin. Hi."

"Enjoying the day, I see," Kevin stated.

Andee inadvertently pulled her little parcel bag and notepad closer to her like a protective mother.

Kevin noticed the movement but made no comment.

"Yes." Andee jutted her chin out as the next comment began to form and emerge before she even realized. "Seems you showed up just in time to distract me from it, too."

"Well, they say timing is everything." Kevin turned to head back to his work. "And I better get on with things and let you get back to your moment."

Kevin continued to ponder Andee as he moved along and reminded himself that patience would be key with her. He was even more determined to break down those barriers and had no inclination why.

Andee sat there pondering her exchange with Kevin. Her reaction to him was not who she was; there was no explanation for it at all. Not one.

The next morning on the beach was a repeat of this scene, and the next and so on. Kevin always stopped, and she was always rude.

After a few weeks, Andee blurted out to him that there was no need to stop to greet her. She was quite happy alone.

Kevin peered down at her on her bench. "Yes, I do," he said, although for the life of him he wondered why.

"No, you don't."

"Yeah, I do." He turned to begin his jog and shot over his shoulder, "even a prickly pear needs a friend."

Andee stood up and shouted to his retreating back. "I do not!" before she realized what she said and then quickly tried to retract it. "I have lots of friends! Damn it! And I am NOT a prickly pear!"

All she heard was his laughter as he jogged further away.

Fists clenched and fuming, she stomped back to her rock stairs and didn't even notice that she ran all the way up them. *What the hell?*

She slammed the door shut as hard as she could when she entered her house and marched up the steps all the while muttering under her breath. "*Jackass, asshole, chauvinistic airhead. Arghhhh!*" she said, all through clenched teeth. She did not even notice a startled Carlita standing in the kitchen.

It was after that episode that Andee decided to change tactics. She would use polite calmness if she came across him, but she changed the timing of her own run. Now she would leave after she saw him run past, at which point she went in the other direction along the beach.

Since she wasn't writing at this point, and there were no deadlines, she felt free to change her time to run. She ignored that little voice within that questioned why she had to change up her routine. Internal conversation would ensue till she reminded herself that he was here only for the two years of his lease, which he was about three months into. That made her feel better. While she tried to avoid him, she would come across him at times when he was finishing up his run and she was returning from hers. He would always stop to greet her and she him, but she kept it very brief and could continue on when she decided. It was in her control again, and when she stopped at her resting spot at the ocean she was happy and calm, for the most part. But the year was moving to the one time she despised, and no matter how much she tried to control it, there was little she could do.

PART III

Gray skies mark the doom
Of unsettled gloom
And oceans rise with powerful might
While colossal winds pick up in flight
The tide has turned and no going back
Its brutal force ripped up the track
The path has changed
It's all rearranged
Pick up the pieces and blaze a new trail
For a new life awaits without fail

The Storm and the Reckoning

CHAPTER
7

As the days melded into weeks, Andee's mood turned inward. Memories flashed and dreams would wake her up at night, leaving her in a pool of sweat, violently shaking her to the core. Every year this happened, and every year she tried so hard to fight it, telling herself that this year it would be different. But the clouds within would gather darkly and hover over her as each day drew her closer to that one day she dreaded.

She wasn't one to indulge in heavy drinking, but on this occasion she would indulge in a big bottle of wine, head down to her ocean spot and drink it till it was gone. This year she decided on two bottles, and she would share it with someone. Anyone would do, and Kevin came to mind. Although she did question why, she decided she would not analyze it. It didn't matter. He was the one in close proximity.

Showering, she tried to decide what she was going to wear. By the time the shower was done she didn't care anymore and pulled on the first shirt and jeans she found. The shirt was, ironically, a very bright coral, which did not match how she felt.

Combing her hair back in a quick ponytail she considered makeup and quickly decided she wasn't going to bother. She wasn't trying to make a good impression; she snorted at that thought. Nope. Nor was she trying to change the impression she had already made. She just wanted someone to help her through this night.

It was getting on in the evening and dusk had already settled in, changing the landscape from sun-kissed curves of colour and contrast to darkness and mysterious shadows of the unseen. She picked up both bottles and started down her steps toward the beach so she could cut across the sand to get to Kevin's house. She could see it up in the distance, and the lights were shining brightly. Beckoning her as a moth to a candle. He was home. *Good*, she thought as she made her way. Halfway there she realized she was barefoot. How could she forget to put her sandals on? Then she reminded herself it was the California coastline. Shoes and sandals need not be worn.

For a moment she debated on whether she should go back for them then decided that if she did, she wouldn't come back. She paused momentarily, listening to the night. The sounds of the crashing waves seemed to echo in her heart. They both sounded so lonely to her. *Thud, crash, thud, crash.* On and on it went, never ceasing. She closed her eyes as her heart squeezed. She looked over at the lights again then decided to continue.

As she got close she could see Kevin was shirtless and moving about in his kitchen, the draperies left wide open.

The last leg of her barefoot journey took her from the path

to a short boardwalk up to the back door. She could imagine seeing Kevin emerge from this very door every morning for his run down the beach.

Knocking, she called out his name and then said, "It's Andee."

Kevin opened the door and his shock at recognizing her clearly registered across his face. "Andee!"

Up this close she was acutely aware of his cologne, which was clean and rugged. Sensual. For a moment, words escaped her while she breathed in his scent.

She had witnessed his powerful body as he jogged each morning, but he was never shirtless. Between his scent, the beauty of his skin over toned muscle and his closeness, she almost felt like she already indulged in one of the wine bottles.

Finding her tongue, she lifted one of the bottles. "I was … ahh … looking to share this with someone and … um … your lights were on."

"I … well … Andee." Kevin hesitated and seemed about to explain when there was movement in the back hall.

Andee looked past Kevin to see an exquisite dark-haired, dark-eyed beauty. Her entrance shocked Andee.

It did not cross her mind that Kevin might be entertaining, let alone the activities they were or had been engaged in until it registered that the woman wore nothing but her birthday suit— as she was without a stitch of clothing. It was painfully clear to Andee that she interrupted more than a movie night.

Andee sucked in her breath in and humiliation, but also found the situation somewhat absurd. She could not comprehend that she could simultaneously think so many thoughts. One clearly topped the others—she was witnessing some plastics surgeon's failure to sculpt his version of double-D breasts. They had completely lost the beauty that mother nature had no doubt intended for them. Once she got over the surprise of the bare breasts, her eyes moved to the woman's face, and the puffed-up red lips were yet another miss for the hapless artist. Andee hoped the woman got a decent discount for the work provided, and while she wanted to laugh, she found she had to fight off the urge to burst into tears.

"Oh shit!" Andee could feel her heat rising to her face and knew it would be a bright red. The urge to flee had her turned and down the boardwalk before Kevin could stop her.

CHAPTER
8

Andee ran. She ran as far and as fast as she could along the beach where only the stars lit the way. She didn't even notice that she was still carrying the bottles of wine until her toe caught on a clump of wood that the ocean had gobbled up and spit back out. She careened headlong into the black night until her face and body crashed into the sand.

"Shit! Shit, shit, shit, shit!" She cursed herself while her body, face, and toe screamed in pain from the unexpected crash landing. She was pretty sure the sand had stamped her body with scrapes and bruises. But all of that was second-ary as she berated herself over and over. *What the hell was I thinking? God, that was so stupid.* She lay where she landed until she realized she no longer held the bottles. Suddenly, it was most important that she locate them. Crawling, she felt around in the sand until she found one and then the other. She wanted, no, NEEDED a drink right now and prayed it was a cheap enough wine that the bottles weren't sealed with a cork.

Fumbling, she felt around the neck of one bottle and found that it had a metal twist-off cap. Finally, something was going right tonight. Tipping the bottle up, she drank as much in one gulp as she could. Then another and another. She would polish this off as fast as she could, and then her plan was to savour the other while she sat somewhere along the California coast alone in the dark.

The next morning the sun did it usual dance along the water as it climbed higher and higher. It played its light across the moving liquid landscape and bounced little slivers of glitter off the highest points of each crested wave. The scene was breathtaking but went unnoticed by the man who began his run along its sandy edge.

Kevin had barely slept the night before and likely would have forgone his run if he wasn't so hell bent on speaking to Andee.

Making his way along the beach, he approached her turf and noticed that the outside light was still on. While he thought that strange, he continued with his run. There was no sign of her at the house or on her bench. He also took note that the water bottle she always left for herself was not there. Funny the things he knew about her in a few short months. As he ran, he scanned the endless line of beachfront hoping to see her familiar slender figure along with her graceful strides, but all he saw was the sand, rock, seagulls, and sparkling water.

He breathed it all in as he moved purposefully along. As he planted one foot in front of the other, he decided he would stop at her house on his way back. It wasn't until he was a good distance out that he saw something further ahead. As he drew closer, he could see the wind playing with it, making it flutter and dance as it swept along.

He peered at the object, as it appeared to be some sort of large bag that was discarded in the sand, and as he drew closer the colour became discernable, and it was a colour from the night before. His heart leaped in alarm as he recognized the coral shirt.

"God! Andee!" He called out to her, his adrenaline pumping more power to his legs, pushing him faster to reach what he felt sure was Andee laying in the sand in a disheartening heap.

"Andee!" He approached and knelt down over her. In one glance he could see the two empty bottles, along with marks on her face, arms and bloody toe that bore witness to what appeared to be a nasty fall. He discerned that the empty bottles had played a part in all of this. She lay on her side and his brow furrowed as he rolled her over. The stench of her booze-laden breath made him turn his head away from her face. She was definitely breathing. Looking back from where he had come and the distance he had to cover to get her back to her house made him swear. She wasn't able to help herself at this moment, and the only way to get her back was to carry her.

"Aw, shit." While he did want to see her this morning, he didn't count on this. He cursed the long walk he had ahead of him carrying her weight. *Well, Kevin,* he thought, *thank your lucky stars she is as tiny as she is.* With that, he hoisted her up and over his shoulder as though she were a sack of potatoes.

By the time he reached her beach area he had switched her

from one shoulder back to the other and back again. His body screamed "no more" while he surveyed those long, winding steps of stone and then the distance back to his house. While his was farther, it would be far easier than the arduous climb up the rocks. It was an easy decision to trudge further up the sand to his house, and finally he was on the path. He could hear her groan and wondered if the way he was carrying her caused pressure on her stomach and created discomfort. He moved her so he was carrying her in both his arms, and his arms protested. He was just about there. So close. Andee's body suddenly lurched forward and with a heave she expelled whatever contents were in her stomach.

Kevin stopped in his tracks as he looked down at the mess splayed over his T-shirt and her chest. He felt his own stomach roll at the sight and the stench of vomit. If he didn't know she was drinking red wine last night, he knew it now and vowed that red wine would be off his list for a long time to come.

Pushing open his door, he set her on the couch, making sure she was on her side in the event she was sick again. He pulled off his shirt and headed for the shower. She wasn't going anywhere, and if he didn't get this washed off soon he wouldn't be much help to her. This was certainly not how he had planned the morning. After a record-breaking short shower, he set about cleaning Andee up. Peeling off her shirt and bra, he washed her as best he could before pulling one of his t-shirts over her head and set about wrestling her arms into the armholes. He wondered if this was what parenting was like. Once she was dressed, he covered her with a blanket and set a pillow beneath her head.

He decided he would work from home today. He sent a

quick email to his top engineer on the jobsite to let him know what was required for that day, and then made himself a coffee.

He would keep an eye on Andee while she slept. He was quite sure once she woke up everything was going to hurt.

Andee groaned when she slowly became conscious, and her body screamed with protest at the slightest of movements. She tried to raise her head but couldn't and she had no idea where she was.

She thought she heard Kevin's voice penetrate the pounding pain in her head. Raising a hand to her head in a futile attempt to clear the fog, she managed to croak, "God, where am I?"

From where she lay on the couch, she could see Kevin at his kitchen table on his cell phone. The moment he heard her he ended his call with a quick, "I just got the quote and am sending it over to you. I'll call you back shortly on it."

"Hey." Kevin stood up and moved over to the couch. Gently pushing Andee's leg from the edge he made room so he could sit. "How's the head?"

"Hurts like a bitch and so does my body." Then the evening came flooding back, and her confusion mounted. "Where am I?'

"At my place." Kevin wore a slight smile, knowing full well that her prickly side was about to be ignited.

Andee struggled to sit up. "How did I get here?"

"I brought you in. Found you passed out in the sand."

"Oh." She groaned. "Not my most shining moment."

"Not your worst, either."

Andee looked at him, puzzled, and he pointed to the shirt she wore. "You lost your cookies all over the two of us when I just about got you back here, or should I say the two bottles of wine you drank."

"Oh God." Unfortunately, she could easily envision the scene and knew instantly that it was Kevin who cleaned her up. She would have crawled under the couch if she could. "I am so sorry about that."

She looked over at him, and with much effort managed to sit herself upright. "I can be such a fool sometimes."

Kevin had shifted so she could lift her legs to sit and to help her as she did so.

"Andee, don't worry about it. Someday we'll laugh about this."

She shot him a look. "Right now, I'm not even close to being there. I better be getting back. Carlita comes here today, doesn't she?"

"It's already mid-morning so you are a little late on that account. But don't worry, I called her not to come in today. Gave her a holiday day. Didn't think you needed to explain this to her."

She closed her eyes with relief and mouthed "thank you" to him. She made a motion that she wanted to get up from the couch. As she struggled to get up, it dawned on her that he was late going into work. "Oh, your work. Kevin, I am so sorry." Again she found herself apologizing.

He shook his head. "Decided to work from home today. I have that flexibility, you know. One of the perks to being your own boss." He grinned at her and stood to help her as she very gingerly rose to her feet. She knew she wasn't going to walk the distance to the door, let alone back to her house. "Can I ask yet another favour of you?"

Kevin looked at the bedraggled vision before him and knew in that instant he would do anything she asked of him. "Sure. Shoot."

"Can I ask you to give me a ride home?"

"Absolutely!" He laughed heartily and put his arm about her shoulders to help her out to his car. As they exited the house, his last thought was that the prickly pear had suddenly lost her thorns.

CHAPTER

9

Andee sat on her bench by the ocean in her private oasis of rock, sand, salt, air, and peace. She breathed in its tranquility over and over and let the calm wash over her. She thought of the events from the day before and knew that she owed Kevin an apology and an explanation. She would give it to him, although she didn't know what to say.

As a writer, she laughed at the irony of it. Words were her life, and she made an incredible living stringing them together in stories that made people feel good. Entertainment, imagination, and sheer magic that was spun with purpose and feeling. If she learned anything from her writing, it was that everyone really only wanted to feel good and happy about themselves. How they did that was a different story for everyone, and if at times they could do that through her stories she was grateful. But what she discovered over the last while was that she was no different from everyone else, and it was time to purge and let go. To finally face up to the truth.

She looked at the little breakfast spread she created along with coffee, which she had brought down to the water. No running for her today, as she had focussed on the preparation of this breakfast by the ocean. Fresh-cut fruit and freshly made biscuits created a light breakfast buffet.

She wasn't even sure if Kevin was out running today, but she took her chances. One thing for certain—she would not show up at his door unannounced again. She gave a wry grin when she thought of it. *Nope, not going to do that again.* She peered far off along the beach line and saw a lone solitary figure moving swiftly. Although all she could see was his form, she knew it to be Kevin just from the way he moved. How, she wondered, could she already recognize the stride, posture, and grace of this man she only met three months before?

As he approached, she knew he saw her and also knew that he would be true to his custom and stop to say hello, regardless of the events from the day before. He slowed from his run to a cool-down walk and made his way over to her.

"Morning! How are you feeling this morning?" He gave her a mischievous, knowing grin.

"Much better." She smiled up at him.

His eyes surveyed the food spread as she handed him a bottle of water. He accepted gratefully, taking a good long drink. He studied her over the rim of the bottle. The sudden and complete transformation of this woman was well worth the episode from yesterday, for he found himself revelling in that smile.

"Thanks."

"Since it's the weekend, I thought you might have time to share a coffee and bite to eat with me? I know it's really short notice, but I thought it was the least I could do after…" She fluttered her hand in an "all that" gesture.

"Well, I don't mind if I do." He liked this side of her. Soft and sincere. A chance to get to know her better intrigued him and he wasn't about to pass it up. He sat down on the bench beside her as she poured him a cup of coffee and then one for herself.

"Help yourself to whatever you would like. Oh, and here's a plate." She reached in the bag that she used to transport it all down with.

As he plucked a biscuit from the basket and then some fruit, she started. "I feel like I owe you an explanation."

He turned and looked her straight in the eye. She noticed his eyes were two different colours; one was a dark brown and the other a deep green. When she first saw him, she would have said his eyes were brown. *Details*, she thought, *is my career. How did I miss that?*

"You don't. You know." He too was drawn to a pair of eyes. Clear-cut amber that could surely slice a stone if she wanted. Steely. Clever. Independent—all those traits he saw in those eyes. He took a bite of a biscuit without changing his focus on her.

Andee drew in a deep breath. She nodded yes. She was about to tell him something she never told anyone. The pain of it was so great.

"I don't drink, you know." She looked out over the ocean, but her eyes registered none of what lay before her, so intent was she with what was inside. "Except twice a year." She drew in a deep breath before continuing. "The birthdate of my son Johnathon and the anniversary of his death." She looked directly at him.

Kevin froze in mid-bite. He felt like something punched him square in the gut, knocking the breath right out of him.

"It was just the anniversary of his death. It is the hardest one to get through. I get a bottle and come out here and drink it, hoping that with each glass I finally get the courage to just walk out there." Her gaze moved back toward the ocean and she pointed towards the waves as they rolled in and were sucked back out.

With a motion of her hand in perfect unison with the waves she continued, "Just walk out there and keep going. Never to come back. But then I hear his voice." A tear rolled down her cheek. "I do. I really hear him. But dammit, I cannot touch him or hold him." The frustration of what she felt followed with more tears. Unchecked now, they came quietly, increasing in number. "'Mom,'" he says, 'You mustn't do that. You still have purpose.'" She paused, searching for a moment to calm herself. "I feel him so strongly, and I ask him what purpose is there? I am trying so desperately to find it, but it is elusive." Her lips quivered as the tears spilled over them and down past her chin. Some rolled under and others fell onto her T-shirt.

Kevin sat utterly still, barely breathing as she spoke. Somehow he instinctively knew that if he moved even in the slightest way it would shatter what needed to come out and he would lose her. He focussed on his heart and felt its pounding increasing in force until it almost deafened him, and he fought to stay motionless. He wanted to reach out and hold her. But right now, it was so very important for her to release it, all of it. On her own.

"Fifteen years ago we were vacationing here, and he sat right there. In that spot." She pointed to the side of the bench

Kevin sat on. "Talking about university. Such a bright young man. He was only nineteen when he died. He and his girlfriend were just going to the movies. She was so sweet too. They were hit head on. Someone lost control, you see. Apparently, speed was a factor."

She shifted her weight before continuing. "Then ... poof!" She emphasized this one word with a grand hand gesture. "All of them gone. Just like that. Everything changed. EV... ER ... Y ... THING." She closed her eyes. Reliving that moment. Then opened them, still looking over at the ocean. Kevin had all but disappeared.

"All I ever wanted was to be a wife and a mother. God, how I loved being a mom, and it was taken away in a split second. My only child. Someone else screws up and my son is gone." The old anger rose with that comment and then just as suddenly it vanished and deflated. Her shoulders slumped with the weight of it. It was such an old emotion, and she was so tired of carrying it. "I could hardly get out of bed. Everything after that was a fog. One big haze. Five years of it, to be exact, and then one day my husband tells me he wants a divorce. I knew he had found someone else, you see. He says I wasn't the same woman he married."

She gave a soft snort at that. "I wanted to say to him, 'Yeah? Well, buddy, you aren't the same man I married either,' but then I thought what the hell was the point? He was right—I wasn't the same person he married. Neither of us were the same. How could we be? But he found a way to find some relief from the grief and I hadn't."

Then Andee turned her gaze over to Kevin. "So we got divorced. He got the estate in New York, all the vehicles, most of the investments, and I got this home, our beach house. Which was as far away from his New York home as he could have it." Turning back to look towards the ocean, she sighed and took a sip of coffee.

Still Kevin made no comment, sensing there was more that she needed to say.

"So, I came out here. No longer a mother or wife. I had no skills or training for anything. Took a job at the grocery store but could barely make ends meet and this place needed so much work. It was around that time that I began to run to take my mind off everything and then I would sit here as we did that last day I saw him. I would pretend he sat with me and we would have the best conversations. He would be laughing with me, teasing me the way he always did." She gave a slight smile. "It was the best I could do to keep in this game of life. I had nothing else and no one."

Then she turned to look at Kevin again full in the eye, knowing she was going to tell him something she had dared told no one. But she wanted to tell him.

"Then on the day of my forty-fifth birthday, I had just finished my run and sat here as I always did, but I was distraught as my funds were depleting and I didn't know how much longer I could live here. I so wanted to stay here. I begged someone to help me. My mother, who was already past, Johnathon, anyone who was listening because I didn't know what to do or who to turn to for help. All I had was me." Her gaze never left Kevin's. It was so important to watch his expression with what she was about to say. Her tears had stopped. "And then this calm came over me, and in my minds' eye I could see Johnathon when he was ten and so excited to give me the birthday gift he made me. He sang me 'Happy Birthday' and then said, 'Hold on, Mom, I got you a birthday gift.' I could see him running off to get it and then the next thing I know this story drops in my head. Totally unrelated to anything I was experiencing at that time. Out of the blue, the characters, events, and the whole storyline. So I came in to write. I found myself writing steadily every day after that. You see, after each run, while I sat here the next chapters would just download. Every day a new one would just emerge."

She gave Kevin a quizzical look. "None of them were even in chronological order. I just wrote and wrote till they were all done and all I had to do was put them in order. It was so easy, and I managed to get it published right away too. Financially, I have never looked back. But it isn't enough, Kevin. I want my family. I want my son."

The tears broke through again, but this time Kevin pulled her close and stroked her hair.

Now he understood why she was so prickly when he approached her here. Why she needed time alone. He had not only interrupted her creative time but also the only time she had with her son. Real or not, it was important to her.

"Tell you what, Andee. If I can get my ass out of bed earlier, would you consider running with me? Then when we are done you can come here alone to enjoy your peace and quiet. What do you think?" He smiled.

"You still want to spend time with a crazy lady?" She smiled back.

Laughing, he pulled her close again. "I would prefer that over prickly any day."

"You got yourself a deal." Andee laughed as she added, "I

don't think you know what you've gotten yourself into!"

"I'm willing to take my chances. Hey, would you happen to have another biscuit?"

They sat like that for a long while with Andee curled up on the bench leaning on Kevin. Talking, laughing, and eating, they built a new easy rapport with each other that would continue on for the next few months.

PART IV

Ravaged skies are past
As the last breath of storm
Reveals at last
A vision of form.
In the rising haze
The phoenix screams
In a mighty blaze
It spreads it wings
Once lost in a maze, a flight it seems
Will rise in splendor with new dreams

Friends

CHAPTER
10

Kevin looked forward to his runs with Andee. She was bright and clever and she also had a sense of humour. He loved to tease her about anything he could. Doing a little bit of homework, he found that she was an accomplished, well-known author, and he even bought her books to read. He had never met anyone quite like her and he found himself thinking about her often.

Carlita was quick to notice the change in Andee and had wondered about it until one morning she arrived early at Andees' home. She was in the kitchen when she happened to glance out the kitchen to see Andee and Kevin running together. She paused in her work to watch them as they approached the bench by the ocean. Curious she watched as they parted with a little wave. Her brows knit together as she puzzled over what she had witnessed. Somewhat disappointed for all she got was a wave. She had been sure that there was a spark between them and she had to admit that she was looking forward to seeing something more than a wave.

Andee was jogging back with Kevin on one of their morning runs. It happened to be one of those rare times when the sun was edged out by cloud cover that was heavy with dampness. The moisture from those clouds filtered through the air in the form of the tiniest droplets of drizzle.

Both were wet from the slight rain and their own sweat, although Andee barely noticed as she was deep in thought. Christmas was only a few weeks away and she wondered what Kevin's plans were. She wanted to invite him for dinner on Christmas Day. It was something that had crossed her mind countless times. She wanted to stay here this Christmas. Normally, she flew back to New York and spent it with Carl and Carol. It had become a tradition that she enjoyed as best as she could, but this year she wanted to stay if Kevin was going to be here.

She decided to bring it up instead of just mulling it over. "Kevin, will you be leaving over the Christmas holidays?" She glanced over at him as she spoke and then focussed her attention back to the sandy terrain.

Unbeknownst to both runners, their bodies moved in unison. Right foot matched right foot as each pushed off. Their arms pumped forward motion together as though they were one unit.

"No, I'm staying put. We're shutting down the site for a couple of weeks and I figure I will just take it easy."

"Not going back for any family? Funny, I never asked you

about yours. Your parents still living?" She breathed in deep to fill up her lungs and then released. Soon it would be time for the cool-down walk.

"My father passed five years ago, but my mother is still living and I have no siblings."

"So you're not spending the holidays with her?" She thought it odd that he would not make sure his mother wasn't alone for Christmas.

"Nope."

She was puzzled. His answer was short and clipped.

"Oh." A little taken aback, she didn't think about her next question "Why not?"

It came out before she realized and was quick to apologize. "I'm sorry, I shouldn't pry."

Kevin stopped running and looked at Andee. "No, you shouldn't."

She stopped as well and raised her eyebrows. His tone was a surprise and she didn't like it. The prickly pear popped back out.

"Look," she stated flatly. "It is a perfectly natural question that for the vast majority of the population would be a non-issue. No need for rudeness, since I know nothing of your past." She decided she would finish the run now and turned, leaving him behind. It never even crossed her mind that she had previously behaved that way herself with this man.

"Andee!" He sprinted after her, grabbing her arm to halt her progress. "I didn't mean to sound short with you." He attempted to explain. "It's just that I don't have a relationship with her. I haven't spoke to either of my parents in fifteen years and I don't want to get into it."

Andee didn't expect that and yet at the same time felt annoyance with him. "I see." She had confided in him and thought they had the kind of friendship that was completely honest. At least, *she* had been.

They were close enough now to her beach area to begin the cool-down walk.

"You know, Kevin." She stopped walking and crossed her arms over her chest. "I only inquired because I was thinking of asking you over to share a Christmas dinner with me, but now I think I changed my mind." She was hurt and knew she sounded pouty but couldn't help herself. She carried on with the walk.

Kevin reached out again to halt her progress. "Really?" he was quick to respond. "I would love to come over." His whole demeanour had changed, and he was now wearing what Andee considered a most ridiculous grin.

She gaped at him and held her hands out in frustration. "How can you just flip moods like that?"

He shrugged. "It's easy really. I didn't like where the conversation was going and now I do."

Andee could only blink up at him.

"It's actually very simple." He tried to explain but she wasn't in the mood.

"I'm not getting it." She sighed, and her irritation ebbed. "So you'll come over?"

He smiled at her and nodded. "Wouldn't miss it for the world."

"I take it you have no plans with anyone?" She was being a little petty, she knew, but she couldn't help herself. They continued walking again.

"Her name is Bebe." Kevin laughed at her. "And nope to that as well. Haven't seen her since you saw her in her birthday suit."

They started to part ways now as she made her way toward her bench and he carried on. With one last look over his shoulder, along with his now-familiar mischievous grin, he flung one more comment before pushing forward. "Just in case you are wondering, there isn't anyone else either."

Andee had puzzled over Kevin's relationship with his parents. She wondered if he went to his father's funeral and if he did why he never spoke to his mother. The other option was that maybe he didn't attend, and that just raised more questions. She decided she would not delve further into it with him. She would let him tell her if he ever felt the need to, but she would not make that same mistake again.

Over the next few weeks Andee busied herself with the Christmas menu, planning and avoided Carlita's questioning regarding her decision to stay in California. Even Carol and Carl didn't push her the way Carlita did as to why she was staying behind this year, and Andee wasn't volunteering any information. Kevin was coming and that had everything to do with her decision to spend Christmas here. She kept telling herself that they had a wonderful friendship and nothing more. So why was it so important to find just the right dress, and why did the menu have to be traditionally perfect? She wasn't looking for the answer to that, nor did she feel the need to. She would let things just be. For the first time in a long time she felt a peace that settled over her being.

CHAPTER
II

Christmas morning dawned beautifully and Andee felt like a little girl all over again. There was an excitement within that she could hardly contain. All she could do was compare it to the belief that magic happened in the night and Santa came to stock up the stockings and leave her a present. She wanted to bounce down the stairs to the tree and see what was there. She knew, of course, that everything in her house would be the same as it was the night before, but still, she could feel that enchanting excitement from her childhood. She felt wonderful as she bounced out of bed.

Kevin was to come mid-morning and the plan was to spend the day together. He would bring some fixings for their morning brunch and she was to prepare the Christmas dinner. Her intent was to start early with her preparations and have everything done and oven ready before Kevin arrived. This time it was a pleasure and she took her time preparing a small turkey with all the trimmings. The mere task of making a meal for someone else provided her with a sense of satisfaction she hadn't known for a long time.

It was something she hadn't done since Johnathon was

living. She thought of her son and gave herself a hug. She propelled herself back in time and saw Christmases past where he was a little boy and she felt his excitement. She could feel him now and knew he was with her in this moment, feeling her own enthusiasm. The old melancholy she usually felt on this day was gone, and her memories brought her joy. No longer did she think of what might have been and could no longer be. She just revelled in the fact that it was, and she could call it up anytime she chose. For the first time in years she felt free.

She thought of Kevin as she brushed her teeth and tied her hair back. Yesterday Kevin laughingly set rules for today. She rolled her eyes as she thought of them. PJs were to be worn in the morning for brunch and during the gift exchange; gifts that they were not allowed to purchase but had to be creative and have meaning. Then and only then could they get dressed for the afternoon for a nice long walk along the beach. No running today. Maybe a game of Scrabble if they were so inclined but they would decide as the day progressed. Dinner was to be a more formal affair and he was bringing clothes to change into. The final rule he laid down, and the only one he insisted upon as non-negotiable, was that there was absolutely no red wine allowed. She smiled at that.

She worked diligently in the early morning to finish her preparations and had coffee brewing when the doorbell rang. Opening the door, she saw Kevin wearing a Santa hat and his PJs. His car was parked in the driveway and he had his hands full with a small present, a tote bag that had the brunch fixings, and a duffle bag with his change of clothes.

"Merry Christmas, Andee!" His grin worked its charm on her and she responded with a warm smile.

"Merry Christmas to you too, Kevin!" She took the tote. "Let me help you with that. I'll just take it to the kitchen. Come on in, and don't worry about your shoes." She look down at this feet and with a slight pause added, "or slippers."

"I have coffee on." She led the way into the kitchen and set the tote on the counter. "I take it this is the brunch?"

He nodded. "Where can I take this? It's my clothes." He indicated the duffle bag.

"I have a spare room on the main floor here just down the hall. One door past the washroom on the right."

Kevin disappeared down the hall and Andee busied herself with pulling down a couple of mugs for the coffee.

She was just taking cream from the fridge when he got back to the kitchen. "Coffee?"

"That would be great." He came up behind her and pulled her close. "Thank you for this, Andee. I got up this morning feeling like a kid again."

She gave him a warm embrace and then moved away. "I can say the exact same thing, you know." His arms around her made her feel momentarily unsure of herself and them. Just what were they, anyway?

He went over to the tote and started pulling out the contents of the brunch.

"I got all this ready yesterday, so it just needs to be warmed up. I was thinking if we just shove it in the oven we can sit, relax, and open our gifts."

Andee agreed and helped him out. "Well, a man that cooks. Look at all this! Bacon, sausage, biscuits, oh, and some fresh fruit."

"Well, I'm pretty handy in the kitchen. Actually, I like to

cook. It's my way of relaxing."

"It looks amazing. Thank you." She smiled.

Once they were done in the kitchen they naturally cozied up on the couch. She leaned in on him with her legs extended along the length of the sofa. They sat sipping coffee.

He handed her his gift, which she found was small and heavy. Opening it, she discovered a fossil of a shell. It was large enough that it covered the palm of her hand, stretching beyond over her fingers.

"Kevin, this is amazing and beautiful. Where did you find this?"

"I found it on the job site here in town about two months ago. It is an ammonite fossil shell. They believed they existed some two-hundred million years ago. Supposedly, they are pretty common around the world. This is the first one I came across, though. When I found it, I actually thought of you and I wanted you to have it. I think of it as though it were timeless. Like you."

"Thank you so much." She smiled at him and squeezed his hand. "This means so very much to me. Especially that you thought of me when you found it."

She reached for his present. "I put a lot of thought into this. I hope it conveys to you how important you are to me."

He opened his present to find that it held a cloth scroll. The ends were made from beach wood gathered from the ocean's edge. All the rough edges had been smoothed from the continuous pounding of the sand and surf. Attached to the ocean art was a large, woven, unbleached cotton fabric rolled from end to end until the ends met in the middle. A ribbon held it secure. Gently, he loosened the ribbon and rolled it open to read what was written within. He could tell that the letters were carefully hand painted in the old art form of script. He read the poem detailed on the cloth. It was simple, to the point, and so much Andee.

My freedom came to be
When you became my friend.
You did not run but held my hand
While I stumbled to be me.
My prickles and quirks you take in stride,
My pillar in this land.
Know, my friend,
That I am there and will return
My hand.
Andee

Kevin read the words over and over while he tried to form his own words of thanks. His throat was constricted and would not comply, and he found his vision was blurred. He sat there for a moment to rein in the emotions that shockingly erupted. But there was no way to pull them in, as they were out of control. The best he could do was pull her tightly to him and hold on as though she were his life raft till that wave of emotion abated.

Finally, when he could speak, the words came out haltingly and full of emotion. "Thank you, Andee. This means more than you know."

They sat for a while longer before Kevin nudged Andee. "You hungry yet?" Once he had composed himself, the playful part of him sprung forth, while his belly grumbled. "Or should I say are you courageous enough to dare eat the food I prepared?"

Andee smiled. "Well, I will eat yours if you eat mine!"

Kevin rose and extended his hand to her. She reached out her hand and allowed him to pull her up on her feet and pull her close. She could feel the whole length of his hard body and could feel her body physically respond to him.

The playful smile he wore only moments before vanished and was replaced by a smoldering intensity that both could no longer deny.

"I want you so much, Andee, it almost hurts." His lips brushed hers while she closed her eyes and nodded. Yes, she understood, and she now knew she felt the same towards him. "But I want to take this day slowly. I want you to have time to think about whether this is what you want as well. Are okay with that? I have wanted you since that first day I saw you in the grocery store, so a few more hours won't break me."

She wasn't sure she could wait that long now that she knew he felt the same way she did. But she decided she would comply. It seemed important to him that she had time to think about it. *God*, she thought, as she opened her eyes. It was going to be a long day if she kept thinking about it.

"Okay, Kevin. We will do it your way. Let's go eat!" At least that would take her mind off this burning desire they both admitted to.

After their brunch they spent the afternoon with a leisurely stroll along the beach, and it was a natural impulse for Kevin to grab Andee's hand as they walked.

She revelled in the feel of the moment. Everything was in overdrive. Every touch, look, smile, scent, tone, and that chemistry that hovered dangerously, ready to combust. All of it was stimulating her five senses and then some. Control was there by a thread that was slowly unravelling with each passing second. The physicality was prominent, and for the first time ever she had to admit to the animal within that she never knew existed.

She already knew Kevin to be a friend like no other. Holding his hand and resting her head upon his shoulder felt so right, and him stopping frequently to brush his lips on her was as natural as taking a step. She thought of him as her "noble friend"—one that would always be there now that she found him. She loved him. Pure and simple. She always had.

But this physical dance that was ensuing between them she knew would have to have its way. The friendship was separate and yet part of all of it. The outcome of this physical release would be the true test of this friendship, and she would accept the result whether she liked it or not.

They paused many times during their walk to watch the waves, point to something interesting, and just revel in the day. When they finally made their way back up the steps to Andee's, they found they had walked for just over three hours.

"What do you feel like doing now?" Kevin asked as they came inside. There was still a lot of time before they needed to finish the final preparations for dinner, as everything was ready to go and the turkey was already in the oven cooking. Andee had set it to a timer.

Andee looked up at Kevin laughing. "I thought you had the itinerary organized for this day."

"I do, actually. How about a movie?"

"Well, okay, I'm game for it. Let's see what's on." Andee

ventured into the living room and Kevin disappeared to the spare room where he put his bag.

Confused, Andee looked over her shoulder to see Kevin emerge with a DVD in his hand.

"You brought a movie?" Andee was surprised he would think to do that.

"Yeah, well. I have a confession. I watch this movie every Christmas, and it really wouldn't be Christmas without it."

Andee laughed with a bit of sarcasm. "Let me guess, *The Sound of Music*?" She pointed her two index fingers at him as she spoke.

"Nope. Better and older than that."

"No way." Instantly she knew he held *It's a Wonderful Life* in his hand. "Let me see!" Not waiting for him to show it to her, she reached out and plucked it from his hand. There it was— the 1946 classic with a young Jimmy Stewart on the cover.

She lovingly ran her hand over it. "I haven't seen this since Johnathon was little. He would curl up beside me with his favourite gifts, mostly toys, and we would spend Christmas afternoon watching it while he played with them. I'm not sure whether he really watched it or not. But he just stayed with me through the whole thing. I haven't been able to bring myself to watch it since he passed."

"I'm sorry, Andee, I didn't know. We don't have to watch it. We can find something else." The movie reminded Kevin of happier times with his mother and hadn't realized that this might be painful for her. He wrapped his arms around her.

"No. Don't be sorry, Kevin. I would love to watch it with you. It was just something I could not bring myself to do alone."

He nodded. He understood.

Andee took the movie out and set it to play before they both snuggled in on the sofa together. This day was turning out to be very special, and she wondered if Johnathon had something to do with this movie showing up. She smiled and sent him a silent thank you.

When the movie was done, they both rose and moved to the kitchen to put the final preparations in place for their meal before they went to their respective rooms to shower and change.

Andee had found a beautiful red form-fitting dress that was decorated with small shiny silver studs across the low scooped neckline.

The dress was created for small-breasted women whose curves were tiny and firm. The feminine, subtle curves were displayed in elegant, clean lines. To complement the dress, Andee wore a sliver chain that bore a heart-shaped locket. Inside the locket was a picture of a boy and a woman. Her son and her mother, the two people she held closely in her heart.

She decided to let her hair loose and have it tumble about her shoulders, giving her a soft appeal. The gray streak that flowed from her roots near her forehead only added to the overall effect of maturity with a touch of mystery.

She also decided to add depth to her clear amber eyes by framing them with boldly built-up lashes using a touch of makeup.

Unbeknownst to Andee, her usually clear amber eyes burned a deeper hue this night, with slow, smoldering embers.

When she emerged into the hall, she could hear soft music and Kevin came to meet her, escorting her back into the dining area where he had taken care of setting out the meal. His eyes never left her.

"You look beautiful, Andee." His voice was husky and low as he whispered into her ear.

They ate their meal in the dimly lit dining room and toasted their first Christmas together. They lingered a little when they were done eating before Kevin rose and helped her to her feet. He pulled her close. "Let's dance a while."

Their feet didn't move much, but their bodies swayed in unison to the slow rhythm of song.

Andee could feel Kevin's arms about her waist and his whole body as they touched in movement. Closing her eyes, she could hear the soft melody and feel every cell respond to the stimuli of Kevin's nearness. His hands moved over her hips and then up to her waist, slowly travelling up her back, around the front to cup her breasts and then over her neck till his hands cradled her head. His lips came across hers, tantalizing and teasing. Every movement he made was slow and deliberate. She could hear and feel his breath quickening upon her and found that her own lungs accelerated their pace, matching his in perfect unison. The music was suddenly drowned out from the pounding in her head of the rushing blood as her heart sped up in response. Every system was ignited.

She wanted to feel him and let her hands explore each muscle of his torso and arms. She let her fingers travel lightly over his face, lips, and down his neck. They switched direction of their own accord, and she moved her open hands over his buttocks and around to the front. To her satisfaction, he was clearly aroused.

He sucked his breath in. "Andee, are you sure?"

She nodded, as this was the only response she could do at this point. There was nothing else she wanted or needed except what he offered right now in this moment. She was bathing herself in feeling, revelling in it, as it had been such a long time since she felt this passion. This age-old feeling between a man and woman was nothing new, and yet it felt as though they were the ones to discover it—it was so different with the two of them.

When and how they got to that room where Kevin had changed, she had no idea, but they were suddenly there, sprawled on the bed, removing the barrier of clothing to feel the heated flesh on flesh. Moving together as they had been moving all along but now intimately as only man and woman could do. When he finally filled her, she could barely contain the explosive passion that consumed all that had been building to this moment.

This was a day that filled her heart and soul, and no matter how long she lived she would never forget it.

The rest of the week they were inseparable. Every morning, day, evening, and night was spent with each other. They touched, kissed, and discovered each other in every way they could. Their nights were filled with a recurring passion that only refuelled itself with the slightest touch. They spoke of whatever they were thinking; mostly of how they felt now. In the moment. Each discovering the closeness one could have with another human being. Neither of them looking beyond the day, for to do so would take the magic of this newness and put unnecessary pressure on them to try to figure out tomorrow. It didn't matter. Nothing did.

CHAPTER
12

Andee didn't even want to think about the end of the week when Kevin would go back to work and Carlita would come back to work for each of them. If the thought did creep in, she would tamp it down, for with it came an unsettling feeling, one that couldn't be defined. She made sure to enjoy each moment and marked them clearly into her memory to draw upon whenever she wished. She of all people knew that anything could happen and change everything, so she made sure to only focus on her bliss.

New Year's Eve was spent with just the two of them. They decided on dinner out and some dancing and they came home early to ring in the New Year. It was all so perfect, and when it was over and Kevin returned to work, Andee found it to be quite an adjustment.

After the first night he had spent at his house alone, she greeted him in the morning with a kiss as she came down the rock stairs to find him waiting.

He nuzzled his face into the nape of her neck, and with a low growly tone voiced what he felt. "I missed you last night. Painfully."

She smiled in agreement. "I know just how you're feeling."

They both decided it would be better to keep their relationship to themselves for the moment, and most importantly from Carlita. While they both adored Carlita, they also knew she had an overly curious nature that involved needing to know what everyone else was doing, and she also tended to offer her opinion whether it was wanted or not. They needed their time to discover and see where they fit into each other's lives. So for now they decided that on the days when Carlita was expected, they would stay in their own respective homes.

As they resumed their run, the routine of their rhythm and conversation quickly came into place. They were easy and comfortable with each other. At the end of their run just before they parted, Kevin glanced over at his house. He thought he could see that Carlita was already there but wasn't sure. He wondered whether he should kiss Andee goodbye and then decided it didn't matter and firmly planted his lips upon hers.

Andee squeezed his hand. "Come over for supper tonight after work. I'll get something on the BBQ."

"Sounds good." Kevin grinned as he turned to finish his run back to his house before his day began. "I will see you at supper!"

"Have a good one!" She watched him as he ran along, and with each step away from her she had a sinking feeling. As he ran further and further away, distancing himself from her, she wondered if it was an omen that she noticed.

It wasn't sitting well, and her time at the ocean was

consumed with disquieting thoughts. Abruptly, she cut her contemplation short and jogged up the steps to her house. Today, she would purposefully focus on her new hobby, which was a painting she had started, and then later she would make their supper. Beyond that, nothing else mattered today.

Andee decided on grilling shrimp and searing sweet potatoes with vegetables on the BBQ along with a nutritious salad. She wasn't sure what time Kevin would be finished but knew his work usually tried to wrap up around six, so she planned dinner for seven. She busied herself in the kitchen tidying up from her meal preparations and then checked some emails before glancing at the clock. It was closing in on half-past six. She moved to the dining room window where she could see Kevin's house and saw he was on his way in his car.

Andee met him at the front entrance. He leaned in to give her a kiss on her lips and then he wrapped his arms around her. His usual easy demeanour seemed to have shifted and he himself seemed a little off as he held her.

"What's wrong, Kevin?" She could feel a change in him; almost a sadness she could not put a finger on.

He shook his head, so she decided to let it go. He would tell her eventually if it was what he wanted to do.

They each talked about their day, and at the end of the meal Kevin reached out and took her hand. "I don't deserve you." He stared down at the tiny hand he held. "I've been nothing more than a playboy. Chasing women half my age. Ditching them for the next best thing."

"Kevin. Don't." Andee pulled her hand back and brought it to his face, forcing him to look at her. "Don't say that." It came out as a command. This was something she did not want to hear him say. She didn't even want him to think of himself in those terms.

"Where is this coming from? What happened today?" She suddenly stood, feeling a crushing weight slam her in the chest.

"It's the truth." He continued to sit, and he put his hands up to his head. "You deserve better. I am not the man you think I am." Now he looked her directly in her eyes. "I am going back to the city for a while. We've made good progress with the hotel here and there are a few things I need to do there. Other jobs."

He stood. There was sadness in his eyes, and he reached for her hand. "I have thought about this, and you deserve someone better."

"You weren't like this earlier when I saw you on the beach this morning. Kevin, tell me what happened."

"I was reminded who I was. That's it. A man my age isn't going to change, Andee. I would only end up hurting you."

"Isn't that my risk? It's not yours to decide." Andee was getting frustrated.

"Maybe, maybe not. However, I think me leaving for a bit is an opportunity to figure this out."

"I have nothing to figure out. I know what I want, and I want you. But if you need time, then take it. I will be okay. I always have been." She thought about how every man she ever had in her life left her. It started with her father, then her son, her husband, and now Kevin. Why should anything ever be different? She yanked her hand free from his and slammed her fist on the table. "Just go, Kevin. Okay? If that is what you have in mind, just go already! Leave!" She wanted to flee again, but this time she held her ground. No. She would stop running.

Stop feeling sorry for herself. She took a deep breath, made her way to the front door and held it open. She would not cry, she told herself. There would be no tears. Not now and not ever.

Kevin slowly drove into his driveway, edging the car up to the house before parking and turning the engine off. Stunned, he sat there wondering at what just happened. It wasn't something he planned to do. In fact, all he wanted was to tell her how much he loved her. How could he explain to her something even he couldn't define himself? All he knew was she deserved someone who had a track record that was solid. Someone who would always be there to look out for her, keep her from harm and love her. That was the one thing he couldn't do.

For a long while Andee sat in her living room in the dark until finally, in the early hours of the new day, she drifted off into a fitful sleep. She dreamt of Kevin. He was running fast and hard. "Kevin! What are you running from?" Her dream self tried to get his attention but he kept on running. "Stop!"

But he could not hear her, and he did not see her, so intent he was on running. Faster and faster he moved over hills. Up and down he went, his legs carrying him with ease. She tried desperately to catch up with him, but it was all in vain. The more she ran, the further away he was until he was a tiny dot on the horizon. She stopped, as she knew she would never catch up with him. Breathing hard, trying to catch her breath, she bent with her hands pressed on her knees, sucking in the air, drawing it deep into her lungs. Straightening, she tried to peer off in the distance to see Kevin. It was then that she noticed the owl perched on what appeared to be thin air.

It moved its head as it observed her and blinked. Although it sat quietly as it watched her, its interest in her appeared to be of a curious, detached nature. As though it was waiting for her next move. She got a sense from it that there was no need to run after Kevin; that it was not what it appeared to be. He was not running from her. Befuddled, she could see nothing else that would cause him to run so fast and far. The owl blinked again. *See a bigger picture*, it seemed to say, *and look closer at what could be hidden.* She could hear it softly hoot before it spread its wings and soared in the direction where Kevin disappeared. As it took flight, its shape changed to become sleek and lean, shifting its definition to that of a hawk—a brilliant bird of prey that rises above everything. It seemed to reinforce the message from the owl: *look at the bigger picture and the details will make themselves known.*

Andee woke up startled and sweating. The dream was as vivid as any daily event she could experience, and for the second time in twenty-four hours she felt she was given a sign.

Realizing she was still in the living room, she checked the time on her phone. It was almost the time she would normally be rising, and she decided she might as well get ready for her run. Intuitively, she knew she would be on her own this day. When her run was over, she lingered at the beach. Closing her eyes, she breathed in the saltwater scent. So pure and calming the ocean was; it seemed to bathe her in it soothing sweetness. She listened to the crashing waves and heard the seagulls cry in the distance. She refused to think of Kevin, for to do so caused a piercing in her heart. She didn't know where they stood. That was the sum of it. Short and sweet. So she deliberately focussed on the sounds and feel of the ocean. Her home.

She had been there longer than usual before she decided to head back to her house. She rose and slowly made her way up the winding rock stairs and into her house only to find Carlita there, bright and early.

"You not run with Mr. Kevin?" Carlita tried to be nonchalant with her question.

"No. I was on my own today."

"Oh? Why isn't he running?"

Andee shrugged. "I have no idea why, Carlita. He just wasn't out today." With that, she moved toward the stairs to head up for her shower.

She decided she didn't want to talk to Carlita about anything pertaining to Kevin. She had no idea when he would be back. *If* he would be back.

Like it or not, Andee had to accept it.

CHAPTER
13

Over the next week, Andee ran alone and lingered longer than usual at the beach when she was finished.

On the days that she came in, Carlita watched her employer sitting alone at the beach and saw her become a little withdrawn. She also knew what had happened. It was her fault, too, and one day she decided she would come clean with Andee, for her guilt was engulfing her in an ever-tightening chokehold.

"Miss Andee. I have something to tell you." Carlita's expression alarmed Andee.

"What is it?" Andee asked, concerned.

"It's my fault."

Andee shook her head, trying to understand what this woman was saying. "What is your fault, Carlita?"

"That Mr. Kevin left." Carlita clasped and then unclasped her hands, wringing them nervously.

Andee reached out and held the hands still. "Carlita. That is not your fault."

"Yes, yes, it is." She nodded vigorously. "It's all my fault."

"How is that even possible?"

"I saw you two at the beach on my first day back from the holidays."

"Okay, so now you know we became more than friends. But that still doesn't make it your fault, Carlita." Andee was becoming a little impatient, because that made no sense to her at all.

"Well, I was happy, you see, but of course a little concerned because of … well, how he is with the ladies," Carlita fluttered her hands in emphasis, "and I know the hardships that you have gone through. So I told him I worried because of how he is, well, you know … and that he can never, *ever*, hurt you. Otherwise he would have to answer to me."

"You spoke to him about this?" Andee was taken aback. She knew Carlita liked to know other people's business, but she didn't see this coming. "Carlita, that is not your place." Andee wasn't happy with her. "But that doesn't make it your fault."

"Well, I don't think it helped."

"Let's get this one thing straight—this isn't your fault."

"Well, I should have warned you he is no good." Now that Carlita felt better, she continued on with what she thought. "He isn't, you know, and…" she waved a wooden spoon she picked up to stir the contents of a pot on the stove. "He doesn't deserve you. A snake, I call men like him. Slithery." She made a face at that word. "He is no good, I say. Be glad you are rid of him!"

"Carlita!" Andee's voice raised in anger. "Stop! Just stop, will you?"

Startled, Carlita stopped stirring and gaped at her employer.

Never had Miss Andee raised her voice to her. "Well, he isn't any good. Look what he did to you," Carlita insisted.

"Carlita! Not one more word! Not one more!" Andee had had enough, and she lifted her index finger as she spoke. "That man is my friend, and you will NOT say another word against him!" Andee was shocked at what popped out of her own mouth, but it was true.

"How could you say that when he's done what he did to you?" Carlita was shocked. "He is an awful person."

"Kevin is who he is, and neither of us can say that we didn't know what he was like before I got involved with him. It is not 'poor Andee, look at what bad Kevin did!' I am a grown woman and I knew the risk I was taking."

Carlita was shocked at Andee's response. "How can you say that? He has used you!"

"I did this to myself. I did it, Carlita! And I don't regret a thing!" As soon as she said it, she also knew that to be true. "That man gave me the gift to feel again. I finally felt hope, passion, and yes, love. Right now I feel anger towards him, yes. I will admit to that, but I am still *feeling*, and it is so good to finally have that freedom again! I haven't felt anything for over a decade, since that numbness took hold when I lost everything I held dear to me. He gave that back to me and I will never ever forget that. So stop talking like this is a bad thing. It isn't. My pride may be the only thing that's hurt, but that is minor. He gave me far more than he took, and I will never, ever forget that!" She turned to leave but swung around again. "And another thing! Whatever demons Kevin has that made him leave what we have, I hope he makes peace with it, and I also know that I am not at the root of it."

Andee didn't even go upstairs to shower. She got her purse and keys. Giving Carlita a purposeful look, she added, "Don't expect me back anytime soon. And I mean over the next week!" She let the door slam behind her while Carlita stood gaping. It took Carlita a few moments to collect herself before looking down at the food she was preparing.

"Well, that's just great. What am I to do with this?" she shouted to no one in particular.

CHAPTER
14

Andee got in her car and drove down the coast without purpose or destination. She decided she would spend her nights in quiet, quaint spots along the way. Her spontaneous decision to leave with no plan, destination or overnight bag had her shopping for some clothes and toiletries in the first town she passed through, but once that was done she found she was actually looking forward to her time away.

Alone now, she could think about the most recent events with Kevin and ponder what she said to Carlita. There was no laying blame in this, and for that reason alone she didn't feel hurt or sadness. Was it because she didn't look forward in that relationship? Didn't pin any hopes or aspirations about where it was leading? Or that she didn't try to figure out if she was the cause of his actions? She knew for certain that she only took in the moment and how she felt in that time and space. She also knew that she was a survivor and could manage on her own.

Whatever he was thinking belonged with him, even if he

found her less than perfect. She realized that it was his issue, not hers. She felt peace within her for the first time in her life and felt that it extended to age-old feelings of guilt for those whom she had lost. That blame game she had played with herself.

She felt guilt where her mother was concerned. That nagging thought that her mother was alone and endured financial struggles most of her adult life because of Andee's untimely arrival. It didn't matter what her mother had told her. She always somehow felt responsible.

It extended to the loss of her son. Did she do something that somehow the gods were punishing her? Or her husband who left her because of something she was doing wrong or not providing for him? All the guilt was suddenly wiped clean. The actions and expectations of what she always felt responsible for were not hers. She felt liberated and freed. She could envision the chains that had continually choked her finally falling away, and there were no words to describe this release.

It was a cleansing journey, and she just followed wherever the road took her. The further she drove, the better she felt.

The route had her come down #1 through Albion, the same route she used to get to the airport in San Jose. This time she decided she would cut off just down from Albion onto 128 but then on a whim decided to stay at a bed and breakfast in Albion before heading out the next morning.

It was a pretty town, one she had always intended to explore but never took the opportunity. Her previous journeys through this place was always on her way to another destination under tight timelines.

The bed and breakfast was in a beautiful home with

spectacular gardens made of sand, stone, flowering cactus and shrubs that could tolerate drought. The owners were an elderly couple who were gracious and friendly. Their hospitality extended throughout their home with thoughtful details that took it beyond just clean and comfortable.

In fact, she found the town very pleasing as she looked around. The homes, buildings and grounds all seemed to be well maintained and much loved. It was easy to feel safe here, and after checking in and getting settled, she decided to go for a much-needed walk. It was already past three and even though her stomach growled for her missed noon meal, the need to stretch her legs won and she strolled down the street, looking for a restaurant with a shady patio where she could sit out in the clean fresh air.

A confidant would be wonderful right now, she thought as she strolled past what looked like a home for the aged. It was a large, graceful building with arches, gateways and carefully sculpted gardens common to the area. Curious, she felt the pull to explore it and tested a locked gate that kept not only unauthorized outsiders from entering but also residents in need of supervision from leaving without it.

She stood there for a moment before noticing an intercom with a button beside the gate. On impulse, she pressed the button.

A male voice came through the speaker. "The key pad is to the left of the button. You can key the entry code there."

"I don't have a code," Andee explained, leaning toward the speaker.

"Well, you need one to get in," the voice responded in a tone that implied she should have known and that this was

Andee moved her mouth in closer, pausing momentarily to formulate something that sounded plausible. "I just happened upon this home and wondered if I could have a quick tour. I would like to see what this place is about." Andee peered at the intercom and noticed the camera beside it.

"Oh. Then you should come in from the parking lot entrance over by the south wing. Just continue down the sidewalk on your right. When you get to the stop sign, turn left. Sorry. Hold on a sec."

A few seconds ticked by and then he said, "Could you please state your name?"

"Yes. Andee Pearce"

There was a momentary pause before a buzzer sounded and Andee could hear the lock release.

The voice crackled across the intercom again. "Come in through the gate and follow the walkway up to the side door. Wait there. Someone will meet you."

Andee pushed the gate and then made sure it locked tightly behind her before proceeding. She took in the old, graceful columns of the building as she moved closer to the door. Newer tinted windows extended high to let in sunshine and light.

She paused by an offshoot of the pathway that lead to a gazebo garden where an elderly woman sat alone. The woman, who wore sunglasses looked her way and smiled. "Hello," she stated. "You have come back."

Andee glanced around to see if she was talking to someone else, for she had never met this woman before.

The woman spoke again. "You with the amber eyes."

Andee moved toward her. "Have we met?" She tried to see through the darkened shades of the glasses but could not see the woman's eyes. With all the people she had met over the years it was quite possible she had met her as well.

"Yes," came the eager reply.

"I'm sorry, but I am unable to recall our meeting. I meet so many. I try to remember, though." Andee felt at a disadvantage.

The woman smiled and clasped her withered hands together. "That's okay. I prayed that you would come back. Come and sit." She patted the space beside her on the swing that rocked her back and forth in the shaded comfort of the gazebo.

Andee hesitated, feeling a little awkward for she had never been here before and wondered about the clarity of the woman's mind.

"I was waiting for my daughter, you see," the woman said, clapping her hands together.

"Oh." Andee sat down beside her in an attempt to make conversation. From this vantage point, she could keep an eye on the side door for the person who was coming down to meet her. "What is your daughter's name?"

"Oh. Oh. Ohhhh…" The woman thought hard, trying to remember and then became agitated, wringing her hands before blurting. "I, I… don't know."

"That's okay." Andee gently reached out to still the worrying hands. "It is a lovely day today. Don't you think?" She was hoping something neutral like the weather could calm her.

"Yes." The woman smiled again and clasped her hands.

Andee sighed with relief.

"Tell me." The woman leaned in toward Andee. "Did you

find the brown-eyed man who sees green?"

Andee wasn't sure how to respond to such a nonsensical statement. Yes. Most definitely this woman was confused.

She wondered how to reply to keep from upsetting this poor old soul. She thought it best to go along with the statement. She thought of her ex-husband, who had dark-brown, brooding eyes and occasionally would exhibit his insecurities in the unnecessary form of green-eyed jealousy where other men were concerned.

"Well, if I guess you could say yes if you count my ex." Andee laughed.

"Oh." There was a long pause before the woman added, "You're divorced then?"

"Long time now."

"Oh. Well, I thought he was so good for you. You must forgive him." The woman smiled and nodded as if that was a good plan.

A woman came toward the gazebo. "Gracie! You ready to go back inside?" She held the hand of another resident, smiling apologetically as she glanced at Andee. "Sorry. Is she bothering you? I'm not supposed to leave her alone. I did keep my eye on her, though. I had to round someone up." She rolled her eyes toward the woman whose hand she was holding. Gracie, upon hearing the familiar voice, struggled to stand up. Andee assumed the woman was staff due to a name tag that read Justine.

"Gracie, here. Let me help you." Justine let go of the other woman's hand and pointed directly at her while stating. "Tonia, you stay here. I am just going to help Gracie for a moment. Don't move." She was polite but firm.

The other resident nodded.

Andee spoke up. "I'll watch her."

Justine smiled gratefully at her as she moved around to help a struggling Gracie.

"Here, I have your cane. Can you feel it?" The woman brought Gracie's hand to the cane and held tightly onto her free arm. Gracie nodded and smiled as she took hold of her cane.

"Okay. Use the cane. Out front," Justine patiently explained as Gracie tapped the cane around in front of her.

"Ok. A tiny step. Slide the cane along. Can you feel it?"

"Yes. Thank you, my dear."

"Ok. Step. There." Once Gracie navigated the slight step, Justine glanced up at Andee and smiled. "Got it from here. Thanks so much. Come on, Tonia." She reached out for the other woman's hand while still holding onto Gracie.

She's blind. Andee puzzled over the fact that Gracie identified her as having amber eyes upon meeting her. She shook her head. How?

At that moment, another woman came out of the side door, and, smiling, extended a warm hand out to Andee. "You must be Ms. Pearce."

Andee shook her hand.

"I'm Claire Roberts. Director here. I happened to be walking past the security station when I saw you on the monitor. You don't happen to be Andee Pearce the author, do you?"

Andee nodded and smiled. "I am."

"I love your books!" she gushed. "Read them all. Just finished reading *Penny Forest* and I so enjoyed it. And the characters. Such magic! It makes me want to believe that anything is possible!"

Andee smiled and was able to get a thank you in there before Claire continued, "are you researching for another book?"

Andee silently thanked the woman for providing a reason for requesting the tour and latched on to it, for she had no reason herself. Spontaneity wasn't a word that was used in the same sentence with her name. Yet this whole day was on impulse.

"I am. I hope that this isn't an inconvenience. It was spur of the moment."

"Oh no! Not at all!"

Andee was curious about Gracie. "Can I ask about the resident I was just speaking with, Gracie?"

Claire nodded. "Of course. She has dementia, so I do apologise if she didn't make any sense if you were talking to her. Mostly she is fairly good; doesn't wander away like some of them do. Likely due to the fact that she is legally blind."

"She mentioned waiting for her daughter. Does she come to visit often?" Andee wondered.

"Oh. No." Claire shook her head. "Gracie has no family. Never married. No children. No siblings. She is all on her own."

She continued to speak as she led Andee to the side door and punched in a code before holding the door open for her.

"She was a teacher from New York. Apparently a much loved one at that. Been out here for about ten years now. She came to us a couple of years ago. Police would find her lost and take her home. Got to the point that the courts mandated that she be placed in a long-term care facility where she could be supervised. She still has moments of clarity, and when that happens she talks about her students like they were her children. Loved them all dearly. Wouldn't be surprised if that is what she was referring to. Have had a few stop in occasionally when they were passing through." She led the way down the hall.

"You mentioned she is legally blind?" Andee queried as she walked along side Claire. She was still puzzling over how Gracie knew the colour of her eyes.

"Well." Claire stopped walking and paused for a moment. "Yes. Clinically, she is blind. That probably takes its toll on her clarity of mind. She gets agitated at times because she knows she isn't making sense, so I could only imagine how she feels when that happens and she can't even see what's going on. She is a darling, though. A sweetheart through and through."

"Now here we have the dining area." Claire pointed out all the amenities, taking Andee through the main areas and explaining each one in detail. Andee listened intently as Claire described the home and all that it offered. It was as clean and as cheerful as the staff could make it. They offered plenty of activities for the residents to keep them busy and moving.

Half an hour later Claire was wrapping up the tour when Andee asked if she could see Gracie's room.

"Of course." Claire smiled and led her to a room on the first floor, not too far from the nurses' station. "We keep those with symptoms of dementia closest to the nurses' station to keep an eye on them. We want them to be able to walk freely but not wander outside on their own or into others' rooms. Every exit door is locked and needs a code to open."

They found Gracie sitting quietly in her corner chair listening to her television set.

"Oh, you came back! I knew you would!" She happily clapped her hands. "Remember what I said about the brown-eyed man who sees green! He will come back to you. I know this." She lifted a finger to make her point. "He is for you."

Neither Claire nor Andee had spoken when they entered, and this puzzled Andee as she wondered how Gracie knew they were there. Andee gave Claire a look and silently mouthed, "How?"

Claire knew immediately what Andee wanted to know. Pointing to her own ears and nose, Claire silently mouthed so that Gracie couldn't hear, "Sounds, smell and vibrations."

Andee nodded, then spoke aloud to Gracie. "I'll keep that in mind."

"You are a good girl," Gracie stated. "Will you come back?"

Andee didn't hesitate. "Yes, Gracie. I will come back."

Gracie smiled.

Andee was in a deep sleep when the dream began. It was about Kevin, and his form was as clear as though he physically stood before her. His eyes were prominent. One brown and one green.

Startled, Andee abruptly sat up in bed, wide awake.

The brown-eyed man who sees green.

Andee sat on the swing in the gazebo, one foot curled up underneath her and the other one planted so it put the swing in motion, rocking it to and fro. She looked across at the other occupant. Gracie sat quietly, with a contented look on her face. She had remembered Andee from the day before and was quite willing to walk outside with her.

"Gracie…" Andee began, not knowing where to start. There were so many things she wanted to ask after her startling connection in the night. "Can we talk of the brown-eyed man who sees green?"

"Of course, my dear."

"What does he look like?"

"Oh." Gracie smiled that knowing smile. "Handsome devil. Real ladies' man. Except with you. He knew he shouldn't because he was so much older, you see. But couldn't help getting involved with you, I guess. I think for the most part it was innocent. Wasn't it?"

Andee sighed. Kevin was five years younger than she was. Flights of fancy. Now there was a title for a book. She internally laughed at herself and wondered what she was thinking. That an old woman who had a mental illness had answers? To what? Furthermore, what was she even seeking to know?

She patted Gracie's hand, playing along. "Yes, Gracie, it was innocent."

The rest of the week was spent in Albion with Gracie, the trip down the coast forgotten. For whatever reason, Andee felt a connection to this old, confused soul. Maybe it was because it could have been her mother if she had had the chance to age. Who knows? Regardless of the reason, she was enjoying her stay, and Gracie was enjoying the attention. She seemed to bloom more every day, and the strangest thing was she remembered Andee but forgot so many other events and people in her day. But not Andee.

On the last visit before Andee was to head home, she stopped in to see Gracie, who was quietly seated in her corner chair. Andee could tell right away that she was a little off.

"Oh, you have come back," Gracie said before Andee could even say hello. She seemed relieved.

"Yes, I am here." Andee pulled up another chair.

Gracie held out her hands, reach out for Andee. "This time has been difficult too. My poor dear. You have suffered again."

"Gracie," Andee was quick to reassure her. "I'm okay. Everything is fine."

"No. No, and I wasn't there again to help. I am so sorry. Could you ever forgive me?" A tear trickled down Gracie's lined cheek.

Andee moved her chair again till it lined up beside Gracie's chair. This enabled her to hold Gracie with one arm around her shoulders while she let the older woman rest her head on her shoulder. With Andee's free hand she reached out and held onto the trembling, withered hands.

By this time, Andee was used to this poor woman's ramblings and wondered if she somehow sensed that Andee was leaving today. Was that the root of her disquiet? Regardless, Andee was quick to reassure her. "Of course, Gracie, I will always forgive you."

CHAPTER
15

When Andee finally came back home, she was rested and calm, which was a much better place than where she was when she left. She made sure to come home on a Friday, knowing Carlita was not going to be there. She loved that woman, but right now she just wanted to relish coming home quietly and let her thoughts wander where they would, whether it was with Kevin or pondering the week she had with Gracie.

The next morning, she rose early to go for her run and found that she had missed her familiar coastline. She always found this place to be so very comforting. She breathed it in and could imagine her body lifting and soaring as she ran. Her imagination, she knew, was her greatest gift, one that allowed her to live here through her writing. She also knew that her imagination could sabotage her confidence in many ways if she let it, but she would not cave into those thoughts. If they tried to sneak in, she knew it instantly and purposefully switched them to something more constructive. This she had learned over the years of living alone, for she discovered that she would feel horribly lonely if she thought about being lonely, or she could feel incredibly blessed that she could make her own decisions, listen to the quiet and hear the sounds around her. The chatter of birds would diffuse any thoughts of being alone when she was surrounded by them.

So for this day, when her thoughts strayed to Kevin and pushed her to feel sorry for herself, she told herself that she now knew that love had entered her heart and it could again, with or without Kevin. While she missed him, she truly wished him well. She wondered if she would ever see him again and how she would act towards him. When she thought this, she thought of Gracie with her internal jumble and her words about forgiveness.

She turned around to head back, making her way along the coastline towards her oasis on the beach. Scanning the horizon, she could see the sun rising and could feel its warmth. Far off in the distance, her bench was almost a tiny dot but she knew it to be there. She could feel her breathing, steady and hard, as she continued with the exertion of running, her arms pumping and legs moving, bringing the spot into view. Larger and larger it grew until she could see the white of the bench and her house high on the escarpment.

As she got closer she thought it didn't look quite right— something was on her bench. It took a moment to realize someone had occupied it. Not the first time, Andee felt a little indignant that someone choose to use it.

As she approached, she could see that it was a man, for he stood up when she got close. Kevin.

Her heart jumped in her chest at the sight of him. She did not expect this and wasn't sure what she should do or say. She slowed to a walk while he remained standing until finally she stopped in front of him.

Neither of them said anything, both unsure, until Andee finally found her voice. "You came back." She mentally heard Gracie's words that he would come back to her.

Kevin nodded.

"Why?" She really didn't want to ask; she just didn't know what else to say.

He shook his head and offered no explanation. He had tried to figure out what he was going to say. God knows he tried to find all the right words, but still was without even one good one.

"Kevin, I don't understand."

"I want to explain, I just don't know where to start. I thought maybe we could do breakfast. Here. It seems to be the place for apologies and explanations." He pointed to the bench where he had set up a carrier that held some fruit, scones and sausage. He handed her the water bottle she left earlier.

She took it from him but did not drink from it.

"I have coffee, if you like."

She nodded, and he poured some from a thermos into a cup. They both sat down, she on one end and he on the other. Kevin leaned forward to clasp his hands and rest his elbows on his knees. His thumbs spun around each other. Round and round they went while he tried to put together what he wanted to say.

Andee waited patiently, recalling another time when they sat at this bench and he waited for her to explain. She would give him the same consideration. She watched the wind play with his sandy brown hair and noticed he had some gray stands intermingled throughout.

Slowly, he started. "You never knew your father, did you?"

"No." She wasn't sure what that had to do with anything but let him continue.

"Well, I knew mine. He was a brilliant man in business and so very well respected." His lips formed a sneer. "I also knew that he said he loved my mother at times and other times beat the shit out of her."

Andee sat very still. She did not know this and now could understand why he severed his relationship with the man.

Kevin turned to her, his face clearly reflecting the torment within. "I love you, Andee. Like no other. You are a part of me, you know? Two halves that fit perfectly." He brought his hands together, emphasizing the fit. "I tried to stay away, but missed you way too much. In such a short time you have become my best friend, my love and my life."

A single tear trickled down Andee's cheek, but she still said nothing. Again, she heard Gracie's voice. "Forgive him."

"Apples don't fall far from a tree, you know. While I know what he did was wrong, I don't know anything else. What if I end up doing what he did and justifying it like I had no other course of action? Just like my old man?" The pain was evident in his words and tone. "I have managed to steer clear of commitment so that no one endures what she did. But I failed where you were concerned." Kevin wiped the tear from Andee's cheek so tenderly. "I don't want to let you go."

She grabbed his hand to stop him and closed her eyes, gathering a deep breath to speak. "Then we do this together.

You don't have to be your father all over again. His actions and mistakes do not have to become yours. You are also a part of your mother. She is in you too."

"My mother…" He grunted at that. "My mother chose my father over me."

Andee shook her head in disbelief. How could a mother abandon her son for a man who treats her the way he did? "What do you mean?"

"I worked my ass off to get myself financially set so she could leave him. The last day I saw them, he did his usual and I could take no more. I put him down. One punch square to the face. Where he did it to her." His face hardened. "I could have killed him. Had my hands around his throat, and all I needed to do was squeeze them till he stopped."

His breathing became shallow between thinned lips while his hands pressed in on an imaginary windpipe. "But I let the bastard go. Told my mother to pack some stuff and come with me. I waited, but she was bent over him, crying. Shaking her head, mumbling. I told her to come. Now. But she wouldn't. She wouldn't leave him. I gave her the choice. Him or me."

Kevin sucked in a deep breath. "I bet you can guess the outcome of that one. The bastard came out on top. So I was done. Finished with the two of them. I told her that I never want to see or hear from either of them again and left. That was it, the last time I saw them."

"Did they ever try to contact you?" Andee felt her heart tear in two for a family torn apart like this. It did not escape her that it would be the same year she lost Johnathon. In the same year two different families were ripped apart.

"Yeah, they did." Kevin gazed over the water and shook his

head. "But it was too late. I was done with them both."

"Sounds like you had been planning to help your mother for a long time."

He looked back at her. "Yeah, I was. I wanted to protect her. She was used to being very financially fit, if you know what I mean. So I had to build up my business, and I was very successful in doing that. When the time came, I was ready."

Andee nodded. "But was your mother?"

Kevin looked at Andee, confused. "What do you mean?"

"Your mother, did she know what you had planned for her? Did you tell her?"

"No, I … I didn't. I couldn't."

"So you gave her all of one minute to make a completely life altering decision? To leave a man she had been with for decades?"

"What are you getting at?" Kevin didn't like where this was going.

Andee sucked in her breath; she knew she was in dangerous waters but had to keep wading out. "I think you know, Kevin." She said it as gently as she could, pausing to let him think it over. Contemplate it from another perspective.

He brought his hand up to his forehead. At first, he felt anger towards Andee. How could she possibly know, how dare she insinuate that he pushed his mother into a decision she wasn't ready to make? She would have been thinking about leaving him before that, he was sure. Or was he? "Why wouldn't she want to leave him, Andee? Why would anyone in their right mind stay with someone like that?"

Andee shook her head. "I don't know, Kevin. There is only one person who can answer that."

Kevin looked down at the sand. He knew what she was getting at. Emotions were conflicted over his features and he worked hard to contain them. "I don't know, Andee. I don't think I can do that. It's been such a long time, maybe she won't want to see me."

"She loved you very much, didn't she?" Andee voice was quiet and soft.

Kevin couldn't contain the tears that formed in his eyes. "That she did." He couldn't deny that.

"Then I promise you that as a mother she would want to see her son." Andee slid across the bench and wrapped her arms around Kevin while he hung onto her for dear life.

PART V

The simple act to trust
Can change life forever.

The Reunion

CHAPTER
16

Andee and Kevin decided that day to do the two-hour drive north along the coast to reach Kevin's childhood home in the country. As far as Kevin knew, his mother, Sophia, still lived there. They had a discussion about whether they should call ahead to make sure, but Kevin didn't want to do that. Once he decided to go, he wanted to get on with it, because if there was time to think about it then he would never go back. That is what he had been doing all along. Thinking instead of doing. Often, his heart wanted to go home but his head stubbornly refused. The only difference now was that Andee was here to help him follow his heart, as she would not abandon him. This much he knew.

They left right after the breakfast on the beach. This wasn't what he had in mind, he thought with a wry grin. Not even close, and yet he wanted this. Badly. He glanced over at Andee and grabbed her hand as they drove along in his convertible sports car. With the top down, the wind played with Andee's hair, pulling and teasing it loose from the ponytail she loved to wear.

The day was spectacular, and Andee relished in the drive as best she could but she could feel Kevin's tense nervousness the closer they got. He seemed to grip her hand as though to comfort and console whatever emotions were unearthed with each passing mile.

She noticed the scenery gradually change, as the further north they went a little more greenery appeared. Finally they left the coast and drove further inland, and within fifteen minutes they pulled into a long, winding, paved driveway.

Following along the meandering lane, they passed massive blue noble fir trees that stood like soldiers amid a finely groomed lawn until they came to where the drive split to the left and right to form a loop that ran strategically in front of the house. The grand, stately home rose to a full two-storey height, boasting multiple pillars that seemed to welcome visitors upon entry.

Pulling up along the front, Kevin stopped the car and sat for a while as his emotions whirled and twisted within him, making his stomach constrict till it hurt. He felt as though he were at the bottom of a rock slide and every rock held a painful memory that hit him head-on with full force.

He saw his father again from the last visit, his face mottled with a gray ugliness that Kevin had witnessed many times in his life. His words, clear and cutting, were designed to hurt. "You dare to dictate to your mother?" Richard bellowed. "You ungrateful shit of a son!"

Sophia put her hand on her husband's arm, trying to calm his rage. She knew the volcano that Kevin was treading onto, its massive lava brewing and churning, building in rage and power until it could no longer be contained. Its' release only promised an explosive, uncontrollable force.

"Kevin! Please!" she begged her son, silently willing him not to go there.

"No!" he shouted at his mother. "You will not stop me this time. You will not stop me from voicing what I always wanted to say to this bastard!" He pointed an accusing finger at his mother while he blasted at her. "Why do you stay with this prick? This so-called husband that supposedly loves you who beats the shit out of you every bloody time he can't handle something?"

He own rage was cumulating into an equally explosive mountain until he could hardly breathe. "What is it?" he continued to shout at his mother. "A home? Fuck that, I can give you that! You're coming with me! Take this asshole to court and file for a fucking divorce!"

His own fury finally matched that of his father's and the two men faced each other. It would be the final showdown. He saw his father's fist clench and un-clench. Saw the pulsing bulging blood vessels that ran across each temple.

Richard took a step toward his son with a murderous look in his eyes. For the first time, he wanted to lay the beating on Kevin, his pent-up rage building to a whole new crescendo. Kevin instinctively knew that the fists wanted to fly in his direction, and he was ready for them.

"You little shit!" Richard bellowed. "All that I have done for you!"

"Yeah? All you did for me, you fucker, was show me how to beat on women! Give into that rage you like to carry around and take it out on a defenseless woman!" he taunted his father. Willing for an excuse to give back to his father the beating his mother had always had to endure.

Richard would take no more and came at his son for the first time. Sophia tried to stop him and shrieked "No!" as he broke free from her grasp.

Kevin was ready for him. At thirty-five, he was powerfully built and he curled his hand into a weapon that struck out with lightning speed to land squarely into his father's face. At sixty-three, Richard was no match for the power that came at him from his son. All the years of anger, hurt and rage were locked into that one blow, and Kevin did not hold back. He hated his father.

Blood spurted from Richard's nose and spilled from his mouth as he tumbled backward off his feet, felled like a massive oak tree as it crashed to the ground.

Kevin was on him in an instant with his hands closing around the windpipe that aided the life-giving air into his father's lungs. There was no struggle. He could feel the power of this moment where he could end all their misery. Then suddenly he let go and stood up.

Sophia screamed and ran to her motionless spouse. The one blow had rendered him unconscious. "Richard! Oh my God! Richard! Pleeease wake up! Look at me!" She shook him slightly and he moaned.

Panting hard, Kevin stood in shock at what he had just done, and more about what he wanted to do. He looked at his mother. "Leave him."

He waited for his mother's response, but all she did was keep calling to her husband as she cradled his head. Her own hands were now covered with Richard's blood. She removed her sweater to stave off the flow. Tears spilled down her cheeks. The two men she loved the most, and it boiled down to this moment.

Kevin was still breathing hard as his senses scrambled to regain themselves. "Leave him," he spoke again. "Come with me now and you never have to endure this again."

Sophia looked up at her son with a grief buried deep in her heart, for she knew whatever words she spoke in the next sentence, she would lose one of the men she loved so dearly.

"Mother, come now. Please," Kevin begged of her.

Sophia's tears flowed, and the sobs formed in her throat. They ripped themselves from her in great torturous heaves. In the smallest of a whisper, she uttered the words that cut Kevin's heart out. "I… can't."

Fifteen years had transpired from that moment. Fifteen years. He knew of his father's passing when he read it in the business section. The reporters made him out to be this giant of a man whose investment properties opened hundreds of employment opportunities. "He will be sorely missed," one caption held. "They broke the mold," another said. "Son does not attend the funeral for one of the countries' most respected men."

It went on for months afterward.

Fifteen years.

He looked at Andee, and she reached out again to squeeze his hand. Willing him the courage to go to that front door.

"What if she doesn't want to see me?" He looked like a little lost boy.

"Shh." Andee reached out with her free hand to touch his

face. "You can do this, Kevin. You need this. You need to speak to her. One way or another so you can put this to rest."

He contemplated her words for a moment, nodded then exited the car. Andee scrambled over the console to the driver's seat. If he was welcomed into the house, she wanted to give them some time alone to work through the last time they saw each other and the last fifteen years.

She booked a room at a local motel on her phone, and would wait there if Kevin needed her, but first she would make sure he didn't need her before she left.

She watched him as he walked up the walkway and then finally the steps. To her, he looked like a little boy who stood uncertainly at the front door. She closed her eyes and willed him to ring the doorbell.

"Just do it, Kevin," she whispered to no one in particular. "Push that bell." She opened her eyes to see him do just that and then saw the door open. Suddenly there was a flurry of activity and the woman who answered the door calling to someone to come quick. Another woman appeared, and as soon as she recognized the visitor her knees seemed to become jelly and gave way. Kevin rushed in to help her up. Andee could see she was sobbing and inconsolable. Her arms wrapped themselves around him, hugging him tightly.

Andee could imagine the incoherent words that tumbled forth from his mother as he was pulled into the house and the door slammed shut.

She sat there for a moment before driving back to the motel room, knowing that for Kevin this was life changing. She hoped and prayed this was the right thing to do.

CHAPTER
17

Sophia could not take her eyes of her son. Yesterday he came home, and she cried an ocean of grateful tears. Yesterday her miracle of miracles happened. Yesterday she refused to speak of that last day fifteen years ago. But today. Today she must. He came back. He would be ready to listen.

They were out in the garden terrace sitting together. She did not know one could shed as many tears of happiness as she had. Her dark eyes filled with a love that she knew Kevin returned. Her beautiful son.

Kevin watched his mother silently. He wondered how all these years she could remain as beautiful as she did, even though she had aged. The lines and wisps of gray hair only added to her beauty. He felt his chest swell with pride. He paused in thought and was reminded of another woman whose show of maturity only made her more attractive to him. Whose amber eyes could tell the tale of heartache and sorrow, triumph and love. Only years gathered could cumulate in that age-old beauty.

"Kevin." Sophia's husky voice broke into his reverie. She reached across the table to touch his hand ever so gently.

"You came for a reason. To find answers? Maybe peace? But, my son, you need to ask for that which you came." She looked him squarely in the eye.

He looked down at their hands. The emotions quickly surfaced, swirling and painful. How could he express in words what he felt? How could he ask her why? Why would she endure the abuse?

He knew it was never about the money, prestige or stature. She was never the type to seek satisfaction in material possession. This woman had only love and compassion in her heart. When he finally looked at her, he saw encouragement and love in her dark eyes.

Only one word could crack through this swirling emotional storm that surfaced, and he barely croaked it out. "Why?"

Sophia smiled a sad smile as she recalled her husband. She closed her eyes to gather her courage, and once she had, she opened them. It was time to be truthful. About all of it.

"When I met your father, I knew. I knew he was the one for me. There would be no other. So handsome and he had an almost carefree demeanour, but I also sensed there was this thread of unleased danger."

She could see him in her mind's eye. That smile. Oh God, that beautiful smile, and the way he looked at her. They had met in a small shop. She was buying a bow for her hair, as she was to attend a dance with her friends. He stood behind her in line and commented on the colour, saying it would look beautiful on her. He asked if it was for a special occasion. She laughed nervously and said she was attending a dance that evening.

Who knew she would see him there near the end of the evening. He just showed up. It turned out, as she found much later, that he had attended several other dances he knew of in the area that night before he found her.

They became inseparable after that. She loved his sense of humour, the way his gray eyes sparkled with light when they looked at her, and his smile. That captivating smile. At six-foot-four, he was a commanding presence.

But still, there was that thread of danger. Something that lurked in the shadows that he kept hidden. She felt it, like a caged tiger pacing back and forth looking for its opportunity to escape and strike out. It never stopped searching.

It was a small thing that triggered it, and she couldn't even remember what it was, but she did remember that he had grabbed her arms and shook her. He left bruises. He apologized over and over, promising never to touch her again in anger. He put the tiger back in the cage, where it rested for a while before it started pacing again.

Sophia was always aware of this thread that ran deep within Richard. It was almost tangible to her. Then one day she finally got up the courage to ask him about that which lay buried and hidden away. She knew she wanted a life with this man and knew he felt the same way about her.

He wasn't ready to talk of it then, so she waited.

Richard also knew he wanted a life with Sophia; he loved her more than anything. But he was afraid of his past. What it would do to their future. He thought many times to end it with her but knew that he couldn't. He considered himself selfish, but he couldn't breathe without her and he lived for her. He knew she needed to know the truth about him if they were to ever have a life together.

So one night they drove out to the country by a lake. He took her hands and through a stream of tears, this giant of a man broke down and told her of his childhood riddled with physical, mental and sexual abuse from his own father until he ran away when he was sixteen, never to look back. He told her of hiding in his closet in an attempt to avoid his father, only to be found and punished for it. He told Sophia as much as he could endure and prayed that she would not cringe away from him.

Instead, she gathered him into her arms and held him while his great body heaved from his sobs of hurt, betrayal and humiliation at what one man made him endure. He could never escape his past, for it was his father's past and his father's before him. How far back it went he could not be sure, and he understood if Sophia wanted out before she got involved. But she was already in deep and loved him. Would always love him.

When they decided to get married, they vowed never to have children. The cycle of abuse would stop at Richard. Of that he was certain.

"But God had other plans," Sophia said with her husky voice, and her tears rolled unabashedly down her cheeks. "For in that first year of marriage, you were conceived." She looked at Kevin, whose own cheeks were covered in his tears.

He had no idea.

"I made Richard promise that he was never, ever to touch you in any inappropriate way or in anger, and that if that rage were to surface that it would be directed at me. Never, ever could he hurt you in any way or I would leave him. Of that I was certain." She remembered how strongly she felt in her conviction, and Richard managed to keep that rage-filled tiger at bay for the most part, for he truly did not wish to harm anyone.

"But it would surface every now and then." Her eyes looked off in the distance. "Sometimes it only took one word, sight, smell or feeling, and it would surface. Each episode grew in its intensity, and Richard could never remember them. It was like he blacked out when they happened. But he kept his promise." She smiled a sad smile. "He never laid a hand on you."

"No, he never did." Kevin was beginning to see his father from a very different viewpoint.

"Anytime he lashed out at me, all I could see was that little boy in the closet who was trying to hide from the one person he should have been able to trust." She paused at that moment because she could no longer speak. Neither of them could.

The minutes ticked on. How many was undetermined and irrelevant.

Finally, Sophia could push on. "I kept waiting for him to break free from that hold. I thought that if I just loved him enough, that he could heal. He did go to counselling and therapy at my urging, and it helped somewhat. I suppose." She paused again. "Even losing you wasn't enough to help him." Her voice cracked at that.

For the first time, Kevin saw his mother as she really was: a pillar of strength, and he saw her love for both of them. Her sacrifice and endurance to the punishment that began generations before in order to protect any future generations. He waited for her to continue.

"I used to keep up with what you were doing." She smiled. "I would read in the papers the buildings that your company built. I am so very proud of you." She squeezed his hand.

"After almost five years without you in my life, I just couldn't do it anymore. I had had enough of that damned waiting. Somehow, somewhere, I found my own anger and did not see Richard as that little boy anymore but a grown man who allowed himself to indulge in what became a lame excuse to mete out punishment. He had been abused for the first sixteen years of his life and had at that point been free of that abuse for over fifty years, and here I was taking the punishment for it for more than twice as long as he had endured it."

She paused, taking a deep breath before continuing.

"I told him that it was time to forgive his father, that it was such an old wound and to let it go. I finally saw that as long as I continued to wait for him to figure it out, he never would. I had to look after myself now."

She decided that she was now the tigress. The one who was mighty and could fight back. The one who held all the cards. The one who was finished with that pacing tiger of rage. She would finally open up that cage. Wide.

That tiger emerged with an intense ferocity. Its anger and rage cumulating in one final act. She did not cower, for she was done with that, and she stood her ground in the face of his rage.

"It is time to let it go, Richard!" she screamed at him. Never before had she acted like this. "I am done! Do you hear me? Learn to forgive him. Let. It. Go! Or learn to live on your own, for I am done!"

"Forgive him?" Richard's face bore an ugly sneer. "Forgive him? That man beat and raped me! And I am to forgive him? What do you know of forgiveness?" Richard bellowed at her.

"You know nothing of forgiveness!" His arm automatically raised itself, its intent to lash out and strike as it always did.

Sophia stood her ground and looked him in the eye. "I know everything about forgiveness, for I have done nothing but for the last forty-plus years. You are the one who has chosen to hold onto the hatred for all these decades!"

The arm came down hard. Its old habit knocked Sophia off her feet. But this would be the last time. The tigress came out and she struck back with precision.

Sophia rose to her feet and turned to squarely face her husband. She spoke very quietly as a calm came over her. "I. Choose…" as she spoke, her index finger poked him in his chest at his heart. With every word she spoke, the finger embedded them deeper into his heart.

"To." Poke.

"Forgive." Poke.

"You." Poke.

"Always." Poke. Poke.

The finger then joined the others to curl into a fist.

"But, I…." Now the fist hammered his heart. "Will no longer endure…" It beat again and again on his chest. "Your fist, or your father's abuse or his before him." Bang. "Ever… again." Her teeth were clenched. "And until you forgive him and all before…" Once more, her fist came out to emphasize her words. "You shall stay away from me."

She finally turned, grabbed her purse and walked out the door, leaving behind her a broken man who only had his ghosts, rage and fist.

Kevin gaped at his mother as she spoke. "You left him?"

Sophia nodded sadly.

"Why didn't you come to me if you knew where I was?" Kevin was hurt that his mother couldn't or didn't turn to him for help.

"Because I loved you both and neither of you understood how to let go of the past. Start fresh. There was hatred in your heart towards your father, and while I could understand that I could not live with it. I had already lived with hatred for too long." She looked down at her hands.

Kevin was about to protest and then realized she was right. Up until the day before, he still hated his father. In fact, it wasn't until this conversation that he found any compassion for that man.

"But your father…" She wagged a finger in the air. "Actually understood all of it in that moment of time, although at that point I was not aware that he did. In his own wisdom, he knew we both needed time to be alone. Time to heal. He had a lot to process, you see. We both did." She paused and smiled a sparkling, beautiful smile.

"After about six months, he sought me out and he was a very different man. He courted me all over again and this time I sensed a man complete and whole. I don't know what he did or where he went in those six months apart. No one could reach him or find him. It was as though he dropped off the face of the earth. But I tell you that I never did sense that thread of rage that always simmered in the background. You would have been so proud of him, Kevin. He never, ever raised a hand to me after that except to draw me in for a hug." Tears welled up in her eyes.

"Not that it was necessary, but I got anything and everything I wanted. Went anywhere. It didn't matter whether he wanted to do it or go where I wanted, we just did it. So when I asked to open a shelter for abused women and children, I got that too." Her teeth flashed in a huge, peaceful smile. She leaned in as though sharing a secret. "I run that now, you see. It has been my pillar since he passed."

Kevin didn't know what to say. He had no idea about his own mother's journey since he left, and he felt small that he wasn't there to help her.

Sophia patted his hand as though she read his thoughts. "It's okay, Kevin. Please do not take this onto your shoulders to lay blame. This shouldn't have been your burden to carry either. I am just as much at fault as anyone. As adults, we have choices, and it is our choices that remove us from being victims or keep us entrenched as a victim. I thought I was doing the right thing, but it wasn't. Not for me or for you. You made the right choice to leave. I was just slower to realize what I needed to do. Who knows, if you hadn't left when you did, I wouldn't have had to courage to finally stand up for what I needed. We had ten wonderful years that wouldn't have happened if you hadn't had the courage to move on."

Sophia stood and laid a hand on Kevin's shoulder. "Richard had something he wanted me to give you. Stay put." It was an order. "I will be right back."

Kevin sat and tried to digest all that she had told him. So many questions came and went from his thoughts. All that he had thought his father was had changed. He saw him very differently; as a person with his own demons and struggles. Someone with deep hurts and scars that needed healing. He saw himself and all his relationships with women and now understood his avoidance to commit to one woman. He had been very careful to choose women he would never fall in love with before Andee. He thought of her and knew she was all he ever wanted.

Her spirit, he realized, resembled that of his mother's. Courage was the only word he could use to aptly describe both women.

His mother returned with an envelope and dropped it on the table in front of him. "Your father wanted me to give this to you at the appropriate time and said that I would know when." She patted his shoulder again as she turned to leave him. "It's time."

Kevin sat alone for quite a while staring at the envelope before he picked it up to open it. Inside, he found pages with his father's familiar writing style. It was carefully and concisely written, and it was evident a lot of thought had gone into these pages.

"My Son.

If you are reading this then that means that your mother has decided it was the right time to tell you the truth of who and what I am. Of our relationship together.

You would know that I did my best to shield you from the ugliness of my own upbringing but you also know in doing so I failed miserably. I want you to know that I loved your mother more than life itself and that I never did deserve her love. I tried to make it up to her the only way I knew how and that was through my work and all its success to give her all the material things that I could. But that could never make up for the wrongs that I did to her or you.

In our last ten years we had what I finally could say was the marriage that she deserved. A husband who loved her and showed her with every action, word and deed.

In those last ten years I never laid another hand on her in rage. You see, son, I finally let that go with your mother's help.

I am not proud to say this, but it was that last time that I raised my hand to her that I saw no fear. In fact, I realized that I never did see fear, nor did she ever cower. She bore her abuse in silence.

What I saw in her eyes was love, and for the first time I saw her for who she was. This amazing lady who was the greatest teacher of all. She who took abuse, forgave and continued to love. If she could still do that after all those years, then surely I could forgive my father for what he did when I was a child. For I finally saw my own father as the abused boy that I was. In that moment, Kevin, the most amazing thing happened. All that rage that I felt all my life just left. So simple. All I had to do was forgive him and I could move onto a better life for both of us.

So now I ask that you forgive me, son, and not for my sake but so that you too can be free of the past. All those generations afflicted with this sickness that we passed along over and over.

Please let that rage, anger and hate die with me where it belongs.

Go live your life with love and happiness.

I love you, son. I always have.

Your father.

As Kevin read through the letter, the tears flowed. They would not stop. They spilled down his cheeks, and the release was tremendous. Liberating. For the first time in his life, he saw his father with different eyes and felt compassion for the boy that had endured the abuse and for the man that tried so desperately to suppress it. He sat there for a very long time before he stood. He saw his mother sitting on a bench in her terrace garden.

She stood up as he approached. He could see she had been crying before he wrapped his arms around her. They had years to catch up on in these two days. Andee would be here in the morning to collect him and meet Sophia, and he was going to make the most of it.

CHAPTER
18

Andee sat at the patio table as the morning sun danced upon all that it touched. The warmth kissed her face, and she relished it. For the first time in a very long time she could say that she felt incredibly happy.

"Andee, my dear." Sophia swept down to the terrace where Andee sat. Her morning dress flowed freely around her while her long hair was left loose to play over her shoulders, leaving one with the impression that she floated when she moved. Andee couldn't help but notice that the woman's hair was still almost black, with only a few streaks of gray. She was still a stunningly beautiful woman whose chocolate eyes radiated the happiness she felt from within.

"Did you sleep well?" Sophia's smoky voice was husky after her night of sleep.

Although Andee had intended to stay another night at the motel, Sophia would have none of it once she found out about her. She wanted to meet the woman who brought her son home and insisted that she stay with them at the house.

Andee had arrived in time for dinner, after which Kevin took her for a long walk to tell her of his time spent with his mother. They decided to stay another night, as Andee wanted to get to know Sophia better. She nodded, recalling the night spent in Kevin's arms. "Yes, I slept very well. Thank you."

Sophia sat down beside Andee and patted her hand. "How can I ever thank you for bringing my son back to me? You who have lost so much, to care enough to ensure that this reunion take place. I owe you so much." Andee looked at this remarkable woman while a tear slid silently down her face. She was unable to respond. Sophia raised a well-manicured finger to swipe it away.

"I knew you were coming, you see." Sophia's voice grew even huskier, if that were possible. "My beloved visited me in a dream three weeks ago and told me an angel was to bring me back my son and that I just needed to be patient." Sophia rose to kiss Andee on the forehead. "That she would be the catalyst to help heal this family. I know a thing or two about healing, and I've found that sometimes to begin our own healing we help someone else find peace. You, my dear, have done just that, and so I pray that this is also a beginning for you to find your own healing." With that, Sophia wrapped her arms around Andee.

Kevin strode down the pathway to the terrace where his two favourite women were seated for breakfast. As he approached, he saw his mother giving Andee a warm hug. Smiling, he couldn't help but joke with his mother. "Hey, now. That's my territory." He laughed. "But I will share her with you as long as you make sure I get most of her time."

Sophia lightly tapped his arm and with a throaty laugh leaned in and whispered into his ear, "I already know that this one is like my own daughter. Make sure you keep her in our family." With that, she said, "Well, I shall leave the two of you alone to breakfast together. You know." She rolled her eyes. "He wants to monopolize all your time, Andee, and who am I to interfere with that?"

Turning, she gave a slight wave. Kevin sat down and watched his mother as she walked up the path back to the house. He looked at Andee with a sad smile then looked down when he spoke. "You know, I feel like I was the worst son to her."

Andee reached out her hand to hold onto his. "Kevin, that is very harsh, you know. You did what you thought was right."

He lifted his free hand to his temple and moved it in a circular massaging motion as though he were trying to erase the unwelcome thoughts that filtered their way in. "I used to think that he was this horrible prick of a father and husband for my mother. I only saw him as this cruel, unfeeling bastard that took his anger out on someone powerless to fight back. I had a great deal of resentment towards her as well for staying. I thought her a coward."

Kevin lifted his head and his eyes welled up.

"I didn't know. You know? I just didn't know. I didn't know he was beaten, and God knows what else. I didn't know any of it." He pulled his hand out from under Andee's hand and held both hands to his head as great, heaving sobs ripped themselves from his chest. Years of pent-up emotions broke free again.

"How could I not know? I lived with them both. How

could I have ever thought she was a coward? All that time she was protecting me and trying to help him, and I made her choose between us. How could I have done that?"

Andee got up and wrapped her arms around him. "You were a child and saw what you saw and formed your version. You were never told the truth." She pulled back to grasp his face with her two hands, forcing him to look at her. "But you are here now. Move forward from this point and don't play the 'what if' or 'should have' game. I've done that myself and it never has turned out well. Let's do the 'look at what we have now' and all that comes with that." She smiled. "It might take us both some practice but it's something we can do together."

Kevin stood up and gathered her into his arms. "I think I would like that, Andee."

PART VI

The journey has been long.
The journey was hard.
The journey made us sweat.
The journey was so far.

The journey got us lost.
The journey had us found.
The journey became known.
The journey was sown.

The journey was sweet,
As it came from above.
The journey was complete
When finally done in love.

The Gift

CHAPTER
19

Andee was intrigued by the shelter Sophia had founded and ran like a well-honed ship. Her crew was an army of volunteers who were mainly those who first passed through the shelter's doors as victims and then later as pillars of strength to help the latest group of victims. Her helpers were large in spirit and strong on will.

While Andee fit in twice-a-month visits with Gracie, she and Kevin had also fallen into the routine of visiting with Sophia on most weekends. Sophia also went their way as an occasional guest. There were times when Andee stayed at Sophia's for the week until Kevin came to visit his mother and collect her. She had grown to love Sophia like a mother, and when she came she had the opportunity to work at the shelter.

So many stories were held within the walls of that home, for those whose lives had been rerouted from one of fear and oppression to courage and independence. Sophia had helped guide and rewire the certainty of many victims who held the belief that they got what they deserved to the conviction that they deserved much better than what they had in the past. Sophia patiently and with grace showed these beautiful people that they too were deserving of fine things in life that included love, security and the right to express who they truly were.

This is where Andee met Celia Henry. Her story was one that Andee could connect with to a small degree. Celia also had dealt with the death of someone she loved who had completely changed her world; but the outcome was very different than it was for Andee.

Celia was a beautiful woman whose dark-brown eyes radiated warmth and kindness. Andee guessed her background to be Jamaican, not only from the colour of her skin but also the slight accent. Her dark skin was flawless, and she almost appeared to be ageless. She wore her black hair short and let her natural curls rule. Long and lean with an athletic build, Andee guessed her to be in her mid-to-late thirties. She only based that on the fact that Celia had two children from her marriage, Jamal, who was sixteen and Georgia, who was fourteen. Their father had been killed in an industrial work accident when they were just three and five. A few years after his death, Celia had found herself seeking shelter from an abusive partner who would beat her for every excuse he had and always blamed Celia for making him so angry that he had no other recourse. She only stayed with him because she had nowhere to go and could see no other way to support herself and her children.

Then one day he let loose on her children, and she finally found the courage to leave. That's how they ended up at the shelter. Sophia helped her get back on her feet, find a job, encouraged her when she wanted to take some courses and most of all was there to support her. Through hard work and perseverance, Celia became a nurse and worked at a local drop-in health clinic and loved her career. In doing all that she had done for herself, she was also one of the main volunteers for the shelter. Not only did she work there, but she brought Georgia and Jamal to help as well.

"If it wasn't for this place, we would not be living as we do. So we need to show our gratitude by giving back, and the best way is to help others as we have been helped." Celia was always quick to remind her teenagers this when they baulked at coming so often. She tried to come in for a few hours on the days that she didn't work, and she worked tirelessly.

Andee found she had a very deep connection with Celia from their first meeting; she almost felt as though they knew each other before they met, which they both commented on.

Georgia was similar in build as her mother. Andee knew without a doubt when she first met them that Celia and Georgia were mother and daughter. Jamal, on the other hand, must have taken after his father, for he was already large in stature and built like a linebacker who easily towered over his mother.

Andee had the strongest impression that he took it upon himself to look out for his mother and sister. He left little doubt that he had immense respect for his mother as well. While he could be the typical teenager, when she spoke to him, he would never argue or talk back and was quick to do as she asked. If she wanted both children to come to the shelter with her, he would comply even when he wasn't always on board and he would jump to his mother's aid when Georgia put the brakes on. However, for the most part, both Georgia and Jamal were happy to help and seemed to know what needed to be done without instruction.

Andee admired Celia, not only for how Celia got back on her own two feet, but how she had raised her children as she had as a single mom.

They were working side by side one day folding and sorting laundry when Celia found out that Andee was an author. She had actually read a couple of her earlier books back in the days when she first arrived at the shelter. They were in the shelter library, and part of the healing process was to lose oneself in something you thoroughly enjoyed. For Celia, reading had been a tremendous escape and helped her to expand her own imagination into something that held hope and promise. The characters were strong and taught Celia that she too could be strong when she followed her heart.

Sophia had come in while Celia was talking about her start at the shelter and mentioned the books.

"Well, you know Andee wrote those books. Didn't you?" Sophia casually added to the conversation, while dumping the dust rags into the 'to be washed' bin.

"What?" It took a moment before the words started to sink in for Celia. "You are THE A.A. Pearce?" Celia's eyes were wide, and her jaw dropped in disbelief.

Laughing and slightly embarrassed, Andee gave Celia a sheepish look and could only nod.

"Oh my God!" Celia gave a whoop and both hands flew to her mouth to stay a flow of garbled words that she knew would not make sense while she continued to gap at Andee.

"Oh my God!" The hands proved to be ineffective, for it

came out again along with more. "Oh my God! I know you? Oh my God! Oh my God! You are AMAZING with those books. Let me touch you!" Her hands flew out to grab Andee's arm. "Oh my God!" She looked at Sophia and blurted, "I know someone famous!"

Sophia burst out laughing at Celia's unabashed enthusiasm, and recognizing Andees' embarrassment over the attention, reached out to loosen Celia's grip and gently pull her back.

"Now, Celia." Sophia smiled. "Look at Andee; you're embarrassing her."

Celia looked horrified. "I am so sorry, Andee. I didn't think. But you have to admit that, it is pretty unusual that we would have someone like you here, you know...folding someone else's underwear." Her sense of humour was like a splash of cold water that had everyone laughing till tears rolled down their face.

When they had all calmed down, Celia became very sombre and her dark eyes grew darker with intensity. "In all seriousness, though, Andee. Those words, those characters and their stories inspired me to grow strong emotionally. They were another building block, along with everything else that Sophia has here. You need to know that, and that I am very honoured that I can thank you in person." With moisture filling up her eyes, Celia reached out to give Andee a warm hug that conveyed all that she tried to put into words but couldn't.

Andee was moved in ways that were hard for her to describe, for she never knew that her writing had any impact other than entertainment. On the book-signing tours she had done, people always praised her work, but she never dreamed it could possibly have had any real impact. She suddenly heard

Jonathon's voice quietly whisper like a breeze in her heart: "See? I told you so. You have purpose."

Lowering her head, she held onto Celia, knowing that something powerful just happened here. She had just recognized that they both gave each other a gift. The feeling was strong that not only was this the beginning of a new friendship, but a life-changing one at that. In fact, if Andee looked around, there were new beginnings everywhere.

Georgia had also taken quite the shine to Andee, and even more so once she discovered that she was a well-known writer. She would chit chat and ask many questions of what life was like as an author. Andee patiently answered Georgia as best as she could, describing the freedom it gave her to live comfortably where she did. She also described her home overlooking the ocean, her morning routine of running alone before she met Kevin and how now they ran together, and of her quiet time when they were done and the inspiration that flowed into her awareness. She spoke of the book tours, how she felt whenever she met a fan, and what it was like to know that her imagination was the greatest gift anyone could have.

Georgia asked many questions, but then it was Andee's turn to ask questions, stating that she wanted to know what made Georgia feel happy. The young girl seemed to glow with the attention and explained how she loved to draw with charcoal and paint. Not long after their conversation, she handed Andee a charcoal drawing that depicted her and Kevin running along the water's edge. In stunned silence, she took in the detail Georgia had put into the drawing, knowing that it was completely from hearing what Andee described. Using her own imagination, she had captured the essence of what

Andee felt each morning when she ran.

"Georgia, this is beautiful! You understood exactly what I was talking about! You've completely captured how it feels! Thank you so very much!" Hugs were a frequent occurrence with Georgia, and this was no exception. The girl revelled in receiving and giving hugs, so it troubled Andee one day that Georgia came in with her mother and shunned Andee.

In fact, it went on for a week until finally Andee had to ask Celia. "I don't understand, Celia, she has done a complete one-eighty. Did I do something to her?"

Celia shook her head. "No. I think it was a Facebook post that one of her friends commented on."

"What would that be?" Andee was puzzled as to how it would impact her relationship with the girl.

"Well. Hmm..." Celia didn't know how to begin but plunged in. "She posted how she was such great friends with the famous A.A. Pearce, and some of her friends posted that she thought she had attitude because she was hanging out with white snobs and was ignoring her friends. Look..." Celia saw the hurt that flittered across Andee's face and put her hand on her arm. "She knows how down to earth you are, that you are a friend to both of us. I tried to tell her try to ignore it if she could, but it is really troubling her."

"I see." Andee looked down at her friend's hand on her arm and grabbed it, comparing the contrast. "Why should it matter so much?"

"It shouldn't, but it does to some people." Celia tried to search for words to make it easier. "We come from an area that is mostly black, and of course there is so much controversy over the differences and such hard feelings that go back generations. There is also the perception of wealth in an area of struggle. But it doesn't have to affect us."

"I know, and I also know that it doesn't have any bearing on our friendship," Andee confirmed. "Would you be okay if I talked to her about it?"

"Yeah, I'm good with that."

Andee was able to find Georgia in the kitchen helping Sophia serve the dinner into big bowls before placing them on the buffet table.

"Can we talk for a moment?"

"I'm kinda busy right now." Georgia was glad of the excuse.

Sophia took the bowl from Georgia. "Well, would you look at that? That was the last of it, so we're done!" She knew something was bothering Georgia and noticed the change toward her once-hero.

"Come on, Georgia, let's go take a walk out back." Andee reached out and turned Georgia toward the exit in a 'we are doing this whether you like it or not' manner.

They both headed to a patio set at the far corner of the yard where Georgia sat with a huff in a grand gesture of defiance.

Andee sat beside Georgia. "You want to talk about it?"

"No."

"Are you sure?"

"Yes." Her arms folded across her chest.

"Well, I know that sometimes talking helps."

"Well, this ain't gonna help or change anything."

"We won't know until we talk about it, Georgia."

Georgia looked pointedly at Andee. "Talking about it don't change the colour of your skin." She was very blunt about it.

"Oh. I see." Andee rubbed her chin. "Yeah, that's not going

to change it. Do you think it really needs to change, though? 'Cause it's what I got dealt with." She shrugged.

"I hate it."

"You hate the colour of my skin?"

"No." Georgia looked at Andee, exasperated, and rolled her eyes as if Andee just didn't get it. "No. I hate that it matters."

"I see. So why does it matter?"

"Because they say I'm trying to be white and I'm a traitor."

"Who says that, Georgia?"

"My friends."

"How can you be a traitor to your people? Aren't we all people?"

"You just don't get it cause you're not black. You whites were never made to be slaves and punished for being black."

"Well, that would be true, and it is something that we can never, ever forget. When I first learned of what happened with slavery, I was sorry to be white. I wanted to be anything else other than white. It seemed that made me somehow part of those who imposed such atrocities to fine folk. But then I realized not all whites felt that way then and not all feel like that now. I know how I feel, and many others agree that we are all equal and deserve love and respect. Colour means nothing and yet everything." Andee grabbed Georgia's hand and placed hers beside it. "Look at our hands. Really closely. What do you see that is the same?"

"Fingers, five of them, knuckles, nails, wrist. I don't see why you have me checking."

"Because mostly we are the same and yet we're not. Our skin colour is just one of the most noticeable differences. We have all the same body parts, and we are all built similar, but if you look really close then everything is different. There isn't one hand that is identical to another; even our own hands compared are different. That goes the same with white people. Not one is the same as another white person and there isn't one black person that is the same, or Chinese person or Native person or Jewish person or Polish person, and no one has the same skin colour, as even that varies within each race. I could go on. But my point is that we are more similar than not because we are all different. It is just how we look at things. Differences do matter." Andee put a finger under Georgia's chin and coaxed it up so she could look into Georgia's eyes. "It's what makes each of us special. We could either celebrate that or use it to fuel something else. It is just a choice. So what are we looking to fuel? Friendship?"

Georgia put her head down. "But I don't know what to do. I don't want to lose my other friends, and I love having you as my friend."

"So these were your friends?"

Georgia nodded sadly.

"If you think of them as your friends, then they must be pretty special."

Again she nodded.

"Well, then, do you think I might be able to meet them and get to know them to?"

Georgia looked at Andee, not sure what to do.

"See, the way I figure it is, if I was their friend as well then there wouldn't be an issue. Would you be okay with that?"

Georgia nodded. She would be more than okay with that, for she wanted to keep all her friends, and nothing else mattered more to her. She wrapped her arms around Andee, giving her a constricting hug that made Andee wince as a rib protested slightly under the pressure. But Andee was happy, and nothing could change that. From the back door of the shelter, Celia watched with relief as she witnessed her daughter's usual display when she was happiest and smiled. Whatever was said, it made a sullen teenager light up again.

Later in the afternoon, Andee had a chance to speak to Celia about it and agreed that getting to know the girls might be the best solution to Georgia's dilemma.

With this in mind, both women came up with a plan that would involve the girls hosting an event where Andee and Celia could participate by working with them. Andee could get to know Celia's friends without them realizing what was happening. But they had to run it past Sophia, as they were hoping to do this at the shelter. First they had to find a cause that the girls felt very passionately about.

CHAPTER 20

Puppies. Kittens. Gerbils. Canaries. Anything furry or feathery topped the list, and so it was decided to rally up the troops at the home and partner with the local animal shelter to raise funds for all these fuzzy friends. They also wanted to increase awareness for family violence and show that there was help for those in need. Sophia was on board.

Georgia's friends were also all on board and were very excited to organize this event. Sophia, Andee and Celia handed the reins over to the girls and they recruited the adults to help with whatever was needed.

As the organization got under way, Andee was quick to recognize the leader of the group. Natasha. She was the one who everyone in the group looked up to and was the big decision-maker for whatever was going on. Georgia wasn't as much of a follower as the rest but clearly adored Natasha. Andee found it was also very easy to win Natasha over, as she had a big heart. Once this was discovered, it was clear to see that jealousy was the root of the earlier issue and she whispered this to Celia.

"How did you know?"

Andee shrugged and with a wry look, said, "I was a girl once too."

As the plans for the fundraiser continued, Jamal found himself spending more time with Kevin when he and Andee visited on the weekends. At times, both found the influx of females a little overwhelming and they would find an excuse to busy themselves elsewhere. Sometimes they would do odd chores around the shelter or back at Sophia's.

Often, Kevin would bring his work with him to do over the weekends and found that Jamal had a great interest in what Kevin did. Drawings of plans were reviewed over and over, as the next phases of construction had to be considered and timed so they remained on target with completion date.

Jamal would ask many questions about the plans and next steps while Kevin patiently answered, explaining the what, why and how such as mapping out the materials, quotes and timing. He even had Jamal work on some tasks, and was stunned with the young man's ability and interest in architectural engineering.

He even talked to Andee about it the Friday night before the fundraising event as they sat on the porch at Sophia's house. "I don't know how he is in school, Andee, but he has a memory that I swear is photographic. He remembers everything. I had him working on a quote today, gave him a quick explanation and next thing you know he's asking me something that we did weeks ago and forgot to mention this time around. He finished it and he did a great job. I only had to change a few things."

Kevin paused for a moment and looked at Andee. "He's a great kid. I was thinking I'd like to ask Celia if I could hire him over the summer break. Of course, he would have to live where we are, but we could try it for three or four weeks. See how it goes. What do you think?"

While Kevin still kept his rental unit, they mostly stayed together at Andee's home. Slowly they were beginning to live with each other without making anything official. They were taking their time, as there was no rush and they were loving every minute of it.

"You know? I would be okay with him staying with us. Maybe Celia and Georgia could come for a bit of a holiday over that time and stay too? What do you think of that?"

Kevin laughed. "The more, the merrier! And if Jamal and I find ourselves overwhelmed by too many woman then he and I could escape to my place." With a wry grin, Kevin rose and pulled Andee up with him. Enfolding her in his arms, he brushed his lips over hers then deepened his kiss before pulling back.

"I think we should get an early night, as we have a big day tomorrow with the fundraiser." Kevin focussed on the pair of amber eyes that looked up at him. He saw the passion that lay waiting and continued. "I have one more activity I would like to do this evening with you, and it can only be done behind closed doors. You on board with it?" He gave her a big grin with a knowing look.

Andee raised herself on tippy toe and brushed her lips over his again. "Am I ever!"

The next morning dawned with Kevin and Andee finishing up their run early as everyone was engaged to pitch in this day. While Georgia and Natasha tolerated Kevin and Jamal finding excuses to disappear during the planning of the event, they had no tolerance for it this day.

The girls were like drill sergeants having the men set up tables for the various products they had canvassed the neighbourhood and school for. They had baked goods, which their mothers donated. Sophia also organized the woman of the shelter to add to the baked goods with their own recipes using ingredients she provided for them.

There were tables with books, dishes, wood signs and plaques that they themselves had created. Old furniture had been dropped off, and there were racks for clothes; there was everything they could think of and more. Recruitment even extended out to their many friends and fellow students to help man these tables.

The animal shelter, which was the main focus, occupied an area with a booth that housed pictures of the current inhabitants. Adding to that, a couple of volunteers brought several of the smaller dogs with their crates that were up for adoption.

Natasha had contacted the local television and radio stations for the free coverage they would supply for non-profit fundraising events.

The girls were in their element and found that their combined efforts paid off huge rewards. At the end of the day, they were able to donate over two thousand dollars to the animal shelter.

Celia was resting on a nearby chair, and Andee caught her eye. Wandering over to her, Andee plopped herself down on a vacant chair. "What a day."

"Yes, I know what you mean. I am exhausted," Celia chimed in. "I think I really need some time off work and *everything.*"

Andee looked at her friend. "I am not surprised you're saying that. Being super mom, plus your work and then volunteering."

Celia grunted. "Keeps me out of trouble."

"Hey, speaking of that. Think about coming out to our place in the summer for a couple of weeks."

"Really? I would love that."

"So Kevin didn't speak to you about Jamal yet?"

"No, what about him?"

"He is really impressed by him and was wondering if you would be okay if Kevin offered him a job to work on the hotel project in our little town."

"Wow! Really? Kevin said that?"

"Yeah, he talked to me about it just last night. He has had him working on some quotes already. Did Jamal tell you that?"

"No, he just tells me that he hung out with Kevin. Doesn't get into detail other than 'guy stuff, mom, you wouldn't understand it.'" Celia did the quote marker with her fingers.

Sophia sauntered over and found another chair next to Andee. "Well, I would say this was a resounding success, wouldn't you both agree?"

Both women nodded as they watched the team in action.

"Yes, so much was accomplished with this event." Celia was thinking of Georgia and her group of friends and all they had benefitted from organizing the day. "Thanks to Andee for dreaming this up."

"'Tis my pleasure. Now all we have to do is dream up how

we are going to get this cleaned up and put away."

As they moved to do the cleanup, Andee couldn't help but notice that Celia really did look tired. "Hey, why don't you leave this with the rest of us. Kevin and I will make sure Georgia and Jamal get home. Okay?"

"Oh, I couldn't," Celia protested.

"Oh yes you can, and you will." Andee would have no arguments with that. "Go home, grab a glass of wine and put your feet up. We got this, and I'm not accepting anything else from you. I will see you when we drop the kids off."

"You sure about that?"

"Yep. Now go. I'll tell Georgia and Jamal what we're doing."

Later, when Andee and Kevin came by with Jamal and Georgia, Andee quickly went in the house to see how Celia was doing. They found her curled up on the sofa, fast asleep. Andee put a finger to her lips to let everyone know to be quiet and went to the nearest bedroom to find a blanket. Pulling it over Celia, she watched her for a moment before heading out the door. She wasn't kidding when she said she was exhausted.

Whispering to Jamal and Georgia, she let them know she would be in touch the next morning before she and Kevin headed back home. She gave them both a quick hug as she left and assured them that they would be back in two weeks. Little did she know that was to change mid-week.

Late Thursday evening, Andee got a call from Sophia that Celia had collapsed at work and had been admitted to the hospital where doctors ran a battery of tests only to come up with a dire prognosis. Celia had only weeks to live.

For Andee, the drive was a long one. So much went through her head as she sped along the freeway. Kevin stayed back and would join them on the weekend, so she was on her own with plenty of time to think.

She thought of the moments after she hung up from her call with Sophia. "How could no one have known that she was so ill?" Andee sobbed in Kevin's arms after she heard the news. It baffled her. No one noticed. No one. Not even herself.

She left early the next morning after a sleepless night and decided she would go straight to the hospital before going to Sophia's.

It was early when Andee arrived at the hospital, well before Sophia was to bring Jamal and Georgia back to visit Celia. Sophia had warned her that it was family only, so Andee patiently sat in the waiting area near Celia's room until the attending nurses cleared. When she thought the last of them had left, she made her way inside the door of Celia's room.

With first glance, Andee noticed every tube that kept Celia in this life. She saw clear tubes that fed from a bag dripping liquid into them that in turn served the needles that protruded from her arm. There were ones that were pushed into her nose to provide the life-giving oxygen that she struggled to intake on her own. But most frightening of all were the changes to the woman in the bed.

Almost overnight, she became unrecognizable. Her body had seemed to have shrunk, and her skin had gone from a beautiful deep, healthy colour to a deathly gray. The dark under her eyes was like a racoon's; it was almost as though she wore a mask of the deepest dark black.

Andee quietly slipped into the room and moved to the far side of the bed where she could hold Celia's hand that was free from the intravenous. She noticed her friend's long fingers were limp and lifeless, and she couldn't help but think of the work those beautiful hands had done. The caring they helped to provide for her children, friends and her patients.

"Celia." Andee leaned in to whisper into Celia's ear. She didn't want to startle her. "It's me, Andee. I'm here for you, my friend."

Celia turned her face toward Andee and opened her eyes with a smile. "Thank you," she whispered and squeezed Andee's hand. "I'm glad you are here."

A heavy-set black woman came in at that moment to check the IV and spied Andee. With a frown, she peered over her glasses as though she were a teacher observing an incorrigible student for the umpteenth time.

"I'm sorry, ma'am, but only family is allowed." The woman pursed her lips together.

Without thinking, Andee piped up quickly, "Oh, but I am family."

"Yes. It's okay." With a weak gesture, Celia picked up her free hand to show it was alright. "She's my sister."

"Hmmh." The nurse gave the two women a raised eyebrow complete with a grunt. Slowly and deliberately, she glanced at their entwined fingers. Clearly the evidence belied that statement.

"My mother married…" Celia paused to draw in a bela-boured breath.

"My father," Andee piped up, finishing the sentence, nodding to confirm the lie.

"Hmm." The nurse's hands went to her hips. "Well, then who was that white woman yesterday who told me she married your father?" She pointedly looked at Celia with a smile. "If you people insist on telling tales, you need to get your stories straight."

"My mother is white?" Celia tiptoed into the question, looking at Andee for direction.

"My father is … ?" Andee hedged.

Shaking her head with a smile, the nurse checked on the IV while mumbling something about what use it was having rules that no one followed before bustling herself out of the room.

Celia and Andee looked at each other before bursting into laughter as though they were schoolgirls busted in a lie. Celia motioned to Andee that she wanted to sit up and needed her to crank up the bed for her.

"It's true, you know," Celia stated once Andee got her settled.

"What's true?" Andee resumed her seat by the bedside and reached out for Celia's hand again.

"That we're sisters. Chosen ones at that, but sisters."

Andee nodded. "Yeah. We are, aren't we?" She could feel her heart squeeze and fought to control her emotions. "We didn't get much time, though, did we?"

Celia smiled and squeezed Andee's hand again. "Maybe not, but we still got to have some, and I treasure every moment of that time."

Andee nodded and found that she couldn't speak as her eyes welled up.

"Don't cry, now. You hear?" Celia gently chastised. "I need you to be strong. I'm gonna ask a big favour here, Andee. I need to know that my children will have a home together. Can you make sure that they do?"

Andee closed her eyes and tears squeezed between the lashes. "I promise, Celia. I promise."

Jamal looked at his sister and his mother lying in the hospital bed before he exited to the waiting room. Andee was down the hall at a coffee vending machine. He made his way over to her.

"Andee." He towered over her and held her gaze for a moment before breaking it to look down at the floor. "I need to speak with you."

He didn't know how to start. There was so much swirling inside. Emotions that ranged from sheer panic to grief to momentary hope and then crushing hopelessness. They found some seats where they could talk privately.

"No one is telling us the truth. No one will say she is dying. But she is, isn't she?" Tears ran down Jamal's face.

Andee nodded but didn't say anything. She watched his face closely.

"I always watched out for her. You know?" He wiped his hand on his cheeks to clear out the tears.

She nodded again.

"When…" A long pause ensued before he continued. "When she leaves it will be just Georgia and myself. I gotta look out for her. I gotta get a job and make sure we still have a roof over our heads. I want you to know that I can do it."

Andee could hear the fear in his voice. No sixteen-year-old

should ever have to worry about such things. The most pressure they should have to endure should be school and dates. She knew what she wanted, but would Jamal and Georgia want the same?

"Jamal, would you consider working for Kevin? He mentioned it to me before your mom got sick."

He looked at her, incredulous. "He would let me work for him? Here?"

"Not here, but where he is working now. Where we live. Would you consider that?"

"I could pay rent for a place for us to live then." He looked determined and a little hopeful.

Andee nodded again. She was thinking more of having them live with her and Kevin, but if he needed to feel that he could take care of things she would let him think that.

She spoke to Kevin that night as they lay in bed together. "Kevin." Andee propped herself up on one elbow. "I've been thinking about Jamal and Georgia."

"Mmm. So have I." Kevin lay there with his eyes closed. "And I know what you are thinking, Andee. I'm on board with it."

"Tell me what it is that you think I'm thinking." She traced a finger in a figure eight over his chest.

"After everything is over…." No one could mention that Celia was passing, not even Kevin. Now, he opened his eyes and looked directly at Andee. "They're coming back with us.

Three weeks later, the four of them packed up Jamal and

Georgia's belongings in a small rental moving van and left what was once considered home to the two of them. Andee and Kevin assured them both that they would still be able to see their friends on weekend visits to Sophia's.

Life had changed dramatically for all of them.

CHAPTER
21

Andee sat very still with her eyes closed and willed herself to hear and concentrate on the crashing of the ocean waves. In they came with a thunderous boom. Over and over. They continued in the age-old rhythm of rolling inland and then being sucked back out. As she listened, she could also hear the cry of a seagull. Then her thoughts plummeted back to the events of the night before.

Jamal was still hurting from losing his mother, and while Andee understood that, she also saw that it was compounded by a fierce anger that he had with the injustice of losing both his parents. The words he hurled at her hurt as he had intended, just before he flipped the patio table where dishes of food, plates and glasses shattered upon impact, as well as the glass table top.

Everyone momentarily froze at the display before them. Kevin was the first to respond and jumped up. Without thinking, he grabbed Jamal by the collar. Over gritted teeth, Kevin managed to speak. "Don't you ever, and I mean EVER do that again." His lips thinned as he continued. "You. Will. Clean. This. Up." Then as quickly as he had grabbed Jamal's shirt, he let it go.

Georgia burst into tears while Andee tried to calm her down.

Kevin looked at Andee and Georgia huddled together and then back at Jamal and pointed to the women. "They don't deserve this." Kevin made a point of purposefully surveying the scene before him before collecting the girls. "Let's get out of here while he cools down and cleans this mess up."

Kevin took his girls into town to find a place to eat. The drive in also gave Georgia time to calm down, as she had never seen her brother so angry.

By the time they got back to the house, Jamal had cleaned up the mess of glass and retreated to his room. Kevin peeked in to make sure he was there but didn't say anything. Everyone knew why he was angry but didn't know what he would do with his anger.

Later, when Andee was curled up beside Kevin in their bed feeling the warmth and comfort of his nearness, she had to tell him what she was feeling. "I love you, Kevin," she whispered.

"I love you too," came a drowsy reply.

"You handled the situation with Jamal really well."

"You think?" Kevin opened one eye to see her.

"Yeah. I do."

"Nothing like the old man?"

"Not even close."

Kevin pulled her in closer and kissed the top of her head. "Thank you for that, Andee."

She thought of Jamal as sleep begin to slide over her, and as her thoughts became quieter she consciously shifted so one more could slip in. Celia. She asked that if she could hear her, to please help all of them cope with the changes that followed in the wake of her death.

Both Jamal and Georgia were still sleeping when Andee went for her run. Kevin left earlier to meet with a contractor before the crew arrived, so she was on her own this morning. It gave her time to try to calm her mind, as the events from the evening before still weighed heavily.

Now she sat watching the waves and willed her mind to quiet. *Listen, Andee,* she coaxed herself. *Hear the waves, listen for them. There. That's one, here's another and the next.* Crash. The waves came in unceasingly, over and over, until Andee was lost again in the smell and the sounds of the ocean. She could literally feel the calm flood over her with each wave. The blessed relief of the ocean. God-given serenity. She leaned back and closed her eyes.

A conversation she had with Celia regarding Jamal and an incident at school popped into her mind.

"Oh that boy!" Celia had placed her hands on her hips as she spoke. "He has no idea who he is dealing with! Him skipping school like that!"

She reached in her pocket, pulled out a cell phone and held it up so Andee could see it.

Andee raised an eyebrow. "His?"

"Uh huh." Celia came back with a grin. "Can't live without

it. My favourite tactical maneuver. Maybe not the best, but it works for me!"

Andee smiled at the memory.

Turning slightly, she could feel the sun's rays spreading warmth over her face.

"Andee?'

Andee's eyes flew open, and she was momentarily startled. It was Jamal. She smiled up at him and motioned for him to sit with her. As he sat, she noticed how he dwarfed the bench. He leaned forward, elbows on his knees, hands together and looked down at the sand.

"I'm sorry Andee."

"I know, and I understand"

"There is no excuse for what I did."

"You are going through a lot. Don't be too hard on yourself."

"Yeah, but so have you and Georgia, and neither of you did anything like that. So I'm real sorry." This time he looked directly at Andee, his dark-brown velvety eyes full of remorse. She saw a lost look about him.

"Jamal." Andee turned her whole body on the bench so she faced him squarely, one leg tucked up under the other. "We've all lost someone we loved and needed. I'm not going to lie to you. It hurts like hell and for a long time. Everyone is different and how long it takes is different."

She rearranged her legs so she could slide over to him, grabbed his hand and lay her head on his shoulder. "We're like a bunch of stray cats that have had their fair share of battles. But now that we found each other, we are a stray cat family." She laughed at that. "There will always be some ups and some downs. But I promise you that we will all be there for each other."

"It's not fair, you know. You lost your son and your friend and we had to lose both our parents." Jamal made no effort to check the tears that rolled quietly down his cheeks.

"No, it doesn't feel fair at times. But there isn't much we can do about it." She paused a moment and looked out over the ocean. "I heard a story about a woman who had two children. Her second child, a boy, was born with a lot of health issues and wasn't expected to live. He lived for just over three months before he died. That woman grieved for her son and thought of all she lost, all that he would never be able to be. Never to become a man and have children. But he would never have grown up the way she pictured. His health issues would have made his life very difficult and his mother's with the burdens she would have to deal with imposed by such issues."

Andee paused to let that sink in.

"What she didn't think of was all the good that could come with her son just as he was. She never thought of all that could be from even having him briefly. God had other plans. Five months after he died, she conceived her third child and eventually gave birth to a baby girl. That little girl was your mother."

"It was?"

"Yep."

"She tell you this?"

"Yep. While she was in the hospital. She wanted me to see that no matter how sad or difficult life is, that somewhere, somehow, good comes out of it. God changed the path and took her brother so the next generation could be. You and Georgia. We would have missed out on three wonderful people had he lived."

Andee looked out over the expanse of the horizon and

nodded, sure of what she was about to say. "There is a reason our paths changed so that we all came together. We don't really know it yet, but it will become clear one day. But I already have my theory."

"What's that?"

"That stray cats don't live long alone. But if they get along and band together, they have a better chance of surviving."

Jamal smiled at that.

"Come on. Let's go up to the house and get some breakfast. I will be dropping you off at the jobsite right after you and I shop for a new table."

They had already reached the path when Andee thought of Celia and the memory of the cell phone.

"Just a question, Jamal. Did you lose your phone?" Andee quizzed him as they negotiated the steps.

"Yeah, I did last night. Did you find it? I even tried calling it with the house phone when all of you were gone but couldn't hear it ring. I figured either you or Kevin had it. Did you find it?"

"No, I don't have it. Maybe Kevin does."

"Well, if you didn't have it, why would you ask?" Jamal was curious.

"Oh, I was remembering a conversation I had with your mother when she was mad at you one day." Andee continued to puff up the stairs. "She said if she wanted to get your attention she always took your phone. That true?"

He rolled his eyes as he followed her lead. "Yeah. Drove me nuts every time she did that too."

When they arrived at the house, Andee got busy in the kitchen and Jamal went to his room to get ready for work.

Within moments, Andee could hear Jamal march to his sister's room and if Georgia's shrieks were anything to go by she had been sound asleep before his intrusion. Concerned, Andee was just about to see what was going on when Jamal came back into the kitchen with a confused look on his face.

"Was Kevin still here when you went running?"

Andee reached for something in the cupboard. "No, he left before I headed out for the run."

"Was Georgia up then?"

"Nope. Why do you ask?" Andy grabbed some eggs from the fridge. "Scrambled okay today?"

"Yeah. Thanks." Jamal hesitated before he spoke again. "I found my phone."

"Oh. Good. Where was it?"

"On my pillow."

Andee looked at him with two raised eyebrows.

"I swear it wasn't there when I came down to the beach! It's got enough charge and everything. And if it was in my room last night, I would have heard it ring because I used the house phone to call it. I even came in here too. Look, even missed some calls from my buddies!"

She gave him a look.

"I swear! It must've been Georgia! She took it."

"I didn't hear it ring when we were out for supper. When do you remember last using it?"

"Right after...." He paused and looked at her, stunned. "Right after you guys left."

Andee knew enough of her own experiences not to dismiss what he was thinking, so she decided to lighten up the moment. She continued cracking the eggs, pulling them open and dumping the contents in the mixing bowl. "So the moral of the story," she said, slightly sarcastic, "is your mother still has her eye on you so don't do anything to piss her off." She took two fingers and pointed them from her own eyes toward him a few times. "Now. Go get ready!"

After a baffled Jamal went back to his room, Andee thought of Celia and could almost hear her laughing along with her favourite, "works eeeverry timmme!"

"Girl," Andee said out loud, mimicking how her friend would speak, hands on hips. "You gotta teach me that!"

CHAPTER
22

Two months later, Andee stood at the window and watched as preparations were being made for her birthday celebration down at the beach by her bench. The people she loved most in this world sent her up to the house to shower and change for the party. Today she turned fifty-six.

She thought of the events over the last year and was astounded at all that had passed. She saw Carlita marshalling everyone to and fro as best as she could while no one paid her any attention. Andee smiled at that. They loved Carlita, yet they all learned to tune her out when her bossy side came out.

She looked at Kevin and her heart filled with love and tenderness. God, how she loved that man. The patience he demonstrated with his mother, Jamal, Georgia and Gracie. Even Carlita.

She looked at his mother and silently thanked her for raising her son as she had and bringing Celia, Jamal and Georgia into their lives. As she thought of Celia, she could feel her presence. She loved each and every one of them with her whole heart.

She watched as a confused but happy Gracie sat perched in a lawn chair while Georgia chatted with her. They were able to get her a day pass for the celebration, and both Kevin and Jamal managed to navigate her down to the beachfront with each man providing a strong arm that ensured her a safe trip.

Her bench now sat just outside a gazebo that each a taken part in designing, building and painting for Andee as a birthday gift. Kevin had been the main architect along with Jamal and both worked hard to build it over the weekends. Sophia had picked out the graceful white sheers that hung between the support posts. Georgia picked the colours and helped with the painting; white on the trim, but the lattice framework just below the supporting rafters between the posts boasted pastel pink, green and blues. It was tedious to paint, but Georgia took charge of that along with some of her friends that came for a couple of weeks during summer vacation. They even let Andee help when she asked. It was a gift for Andee from them all, and she would treasure it.

The gazebo gracefully stood within the nature-made temple of rock. They never moved the bench from where it was originally placed but built the gazebo close by.

Turning, she went to get her things for her shower when her breath caught in her throat and her body physically refused to cooperate. Intuitively she felt as though time had stopped and she could feel herself shift in a way she never knew possible. It was as though her physical body transported itself to another dimension.

That's when she saw him.

"Johnathon!" She called out to him, but her mouth never made a sound.

His presence was almost tangible, and she could clearly see him in her mind's eye. This time, though, he was a fully grown man. So handsome. The youthfulness that she remembered had transformed into chiseled features. He was strong. Charismatic. His dark hair was neatly trimmed and there was an intensity about his dark eyes. She saw herself reach out to touch his face and could feel stubble on his cheek.

She was in shock and stood very still, daring not to even breathe now that she knew he was here for real, for in her mind this was as profound and as vivid as if he was in physical form.

He leaned in close and softly spoke. "Have you figured it out yet?'

"What's that, my son?" She stood there in awe, barely registering that she spoke while no words were uttered from her mouth.

She was observer and yet a participant.

"Your purpose."

She looked out the window at the people she had just been watching.

"My family."

Johnathon shook his head. "They are but a result of it. Try again. Only feel it. Here." He moved his hand and pointed to the region of her heart.

She closed her eyes.

In an instant, everything came together. She felt her love for him burst forth with a new intensity, for she knew she loved him as much this way as she did while he was alive, if not more. In his present form, he had taught her that impossibilities were possible; only with the openness of believing when there was nothing to believe could she find them. The journey she had to take to get here. All the heartache, the joys. All the simple things that life had held for her right down to a single grain of sand. She finally understood it in the split second of a lightning bolt that shot through her whole being.

She thought her heart would explode. "Love." Her intensity magnified with the addition of one more word, and she smiled as she added, "everything."

She saw and felt her son reach out to hold her. Unlike other times, this time she could feel his embrace and she could smell the ocean and knew that he permeated everything.

"It's time to go back, Mom."

She pulled back and reached out to feel his hair and stubble on his chin, still in awe of what she was feeling. There was no sadness in this parting, for she knew he was never far from her. "Thank you," her mind echoed in a whisper.

"I have another surprise for you, though. You will know it when it crosses your path. Let it remind you that I am always with you."

She nodded slowly.

Suddenly, her breathe caught in her lungs and slammed her with a force that made her suck in air as though she had been oxygen deprived. She once again became fully aware of her body and surroundings. It was as though she had momentarily left and came back.

Her legs were shaking, and she needed to sit. In awed silence, she tried to take in what happened.

"Andee!" Kevin was at the door. "Are you okay? I was calling from downstairs, but you didn't answer."

She nodded. "Yeah. I'm okay."

It didn't escape Kevin that she was pale and shaky. "Are you sure, Andee?"

Smiling up at him, she knew she was more than okay but would never be able to put it in words. She stood up and wrapped her arms around him. "I am."

He brought a hand up, stroked her cheek and brushed his lips across hers.

"You go on down while I jump in the shower. I won't be long."

With a devilish grin, Kevin asked, "You need some company and help with that shower?" He pulled her in tighter with a gentle squeeze.

"Mmmm." Andee sighed then gently pushed him toward the door to the hall. She just happened to look out the window and could see Carlita with her hands on her hips and Sophia waltzing away from her. "It looks as though there might be a few feathers getting ruffled down there. Maybe you should get back down there and help keep peace. I'll be down in about a half hour."

Kevin glanced out the window and grinned. "Yeah, I see what you mean. Looks like Carlita has met her match with Mom."

After a quick five-minute shower, Andee found herself in her closet deciding that she wanted to wear for this occasion. She spied one of her favorite sundresses that was splattered with an array of bright-yellow sunflowers and pink-painted daisies while various hues of green foliage livened up a white background. It was definitely a festive dress, and she knew just the sandals she wanted to wear. They were a dazzling yellow pair of flip flops she had bought a number of years before. Searching, she found them at the back of her shoe shelves. Reaching in to pull them out, she inadvertently knocked her briefcase to the floor from which a bunch of loose papers scattered themselves on the floor.

"Shoot." Bending down to pick them up, she wondered what they were, as she thought she had emptied this out from the last time she used it. After reading the first few sentences, she recognized it as the summary of the reading the young woman who sat next to her on the flight to New York had done.

She remembered how upset she had been; she had stuffed the papers in the side of her briefcase and had completely forgotten about it until now. She read the business card that she found amidst the papers. Shelly. Yes, that was her name. She placed the card on her desk.

Curious, she read with interest and was quickly able to recall a lot of what had been described with the first card that was laid out as the Blasted Tower.

She could almost recall what it looked like as she read through the meaning of it. A card of sudden changes, it symbolized striking out the old, worn-out tower with a devastating bolt of lightning that demolished its carefully constructed walls. She thought of all the towers she had come across in her life that were brutally destroyed. Some of them she knew with such crushing force she wondered how she survived it. The last tower she built from ashes served only to maintain a sad and lonely existence that was predictable, to the extent that all she had was herself. It wasn't until she opened herself up to Kevin that its carefully constructed protective walls crumbled this time around. She recalled that she herself had stood in the way of changing her life until she finally let it go and was honest with someone. Anyone. Thank God it was Kevin.

She read further and recalled the heart of daggers. She had been broken twice, from the death of her son and the ultimate divorce. Then the Death card as one of gradual change shedding of the old as a result of the Blasted Tower. *You did not see this coming.* Now she understood this as the building of trust to enter her relationship with Kevin.

"My God." Andee breathed out the words. This was all making sense now. The hairs on the back of her neck suddenly felt like they were small antennae standing straight and tall. This signal motored down her arms to form goosebumps and caused a chill to race through her whole being.

The aim was the Lover's card, and she now remembered thinking of Kevin in that moment. Her mouth fell open. Skimming quickly, she read down to the Two of Wands. Making a choice, sharing what is within. "You have the courage to do this now."

Barely registering, it was suddenly incredibly important to read the last page of what Shelly wrote.

The Two of Cups in the ninth position. Man and Woman. *Do not fool yourself that you are happy on your own. Once you are honest and admit that you can finally open your heart, you will see fulfilment.*

The tenth position was one of coming together as a family. A reunion of sorts. A matriarch and a man and a woman. A boy and a girl, but I see also a shadow of a boy instrumental in building of a family. Yours.

Andee fell into a chair that sat beside her closet door, completely in shock. There was a reunion. Sophia and Kevin. A boy and a girl. Jamal and Georgia. The shadow of a boy.

"Johnathon!" Andee's hand flew to her mouth as his name escaped her lips. In unbelievable awareness, Andee knew what had taken place. Her eyes flew to the final paragraph.

The eleventh card. The Ten of Cups. A card of completion. Family. Spouse. Son. Daughter. You will feel whole. Happy. Eleven months.

Andee was in shock. How? How could she have predicted this? From a set of cards? She sat there dumbfounded. It was all true. All of it.

She remained seated in the chair for a while and remembered what had taken place earlier and a slow smile spread across her face. She could clearly see Johnathon again and hear him laughing, telling her happy birthday and that he loved her.

Quietly, with eyes closed, she let it all download. Once it stopped, she moved over to her desk to write as fast as she could before it escaped her. She then picked up the business card and knew that she would be calling Shelly before she got too involved in writing her next book. She would need her to do the research.

She had one more thing to write before she went down to join her family. This time her new book would start off with a title, and it peeled off her pen with ease.

Picking up her paper, she read it out loud. "The Blasted Tower. By Andee Pearce." She smiled at the sound of it. Turning, she made her way to the door and the top of the stairs where she paused to look up at the heavens.

So much had changed from the year before that no one could have predicted, and yet it was. She had her family and knew the miracle that Johnathon was still in her life and had moved heaven and earth for her.

"Johnathon. Thank you. And I love you with all my heart!"

The shrill of the phone startled Andee momentarily and she raced downstairs to pick it up.

"Andee!" It was Carol. "Happy birthday! Oh my Gosh! You turn fifty-six today! Carl! I got her! Carl! Do you want to know what the meaning of five and six is? Or fifty-six? Don't think we can top that last year, but Oh my Gosh, this is good! Carl, come quick! I got her on the phone! Carl!"

Andee could only smile.